The Tall Girls

a play about
playing basketball

Meg Miroshnik

A SAMUEL FRENCH ACTING EDITION

SAMUEL FRENCH
FOUNDED 1830

SAMUELFRENCH.COM
SAMUELFRENCH-LONDON.CO.UK

MUSIC USE NOTE

IMPORTANT BILLING AND CREDIT REQUIREMENTS

THE TALL GIRLS was first produced by the Alliance Theatre (Susan V. Booth, Artistic Director) in Atlanta, Georgia. The opening date was March 12, 2014. The performance was directed by Susan V. Booth, with sets by Chien-Yu Peng, costumes by Lex Liang, lighting by Pete Shinn, and sound by Clay Benning. The Production Stage Manager was Lark Hackshaw. The cast was as follows:

JEAN	Emily Kitchens
ALMEDA	Kally Duling
INEZ	Lauren Boyd
LURLENE	Veronika Duerr
PUPPY	Hayley Platt
HAUNT JOHNNY	Travis Smith

THE TALL GIRLS was developed during a residency at the Eugene O'Neill Theater Center's National Playwrights Conference in 2012 (Wendy C. Goldberg, Artistic Director; Preston Whiteway, Executive Director). The workshop was directed by Hayley Finn. The play was subsequently developed at La Jolla Playhouse as a part of their inaugural DNA Series in 2013. The workshop was directed by Juliette Carrillo.

CHARACTERS

JEAN – 15 ½, *the strong forward.*

Cool-headed and decisive. A natural strategist. New to the sport.

ALMEDA – 14, *the shooting guard.*

Scrappy, muscular, and temperamental; most likely to intentionally foul.

INEZ – 17, *the small forward.*

Very little natural athletic skill, but a nurturing presence.

LURLENE – 16, *the center.*

Tall and lazy. Unlikely to practice or rebound. A boy-crazy liar.

PUPPY – 18, *the point guard.*

Small – very, very small. A little lady in the making, but a fast, nimble ball handler.

HAUNT JOHNNY

Handsome and much, much older.

SETTING

Poor Prairie, a dusty town in an unnamed Midwestern state

TIME

A mythical moment in the 1930s

AUTHOR'S NOTES

On height:

The hierarchy of height in this play is as follows: Lurlene is the tallest; Jean is also remarkably tall; Almeda and Inez are of average height; and Puppy is very, very short. It will almost always be impossible to cast the play thus. I would therefore invite you to think of tallness as a state of mind, a way of being in the world.

On basketball:

The basketball games and scrimmages in this play will never proceed in the same way twice. That's the point. Embrace the liveness and unpredictability of a bouncing ball onstage.

I would recommend approaching the staging of these moments not as a choreographer, but a coach: Teach the cast a few plays to run as needed. That way, when a shot is missed, the performers can regroup by getting the ball back out to the point guard to call a new play. The stage directions in these sections indicate the arc of the story I am trying to tell through the game or scrimmage; the action described needn't be viewed as entirely prescriptive as long as that story is told.

The drills at the top of Scene 8 should highlight the skill and cohesion of the team. A few drills are suggested in the text, but these may be substituted with others if desired. Think of drills that will keep as many performers as possible in motion simultaneously.

The way each character plays basketball should be an expression of his or her true self.

On language:

The characters speak a musical, invented language meant to evoke a moment in history without attempting to represent it exactly.

For my grandfather and his mysterious,
short-lived career as a basketball coach

Douglas Sommerville and the undefeated 1934
Glyndon High School team (Glyndon, Minnesota)

One

(In darkness, the sound of:)

(A basketball dribbled on hard-packed dirt. Far away, initially, and then increasingly close. Slow, initially, and then with increasing speed.)

(Another ball joins in. And then another.)

(A ball hits a wooden backboard and rolls around a metal rim and back onto the dirt.)

(Another ball follows. And then another – all the while dribbling continues to create a thunderstorm of basketball.)

(A whistle flutters, futile, under the pounding of basketballs on wood and dirt and metal.)

(The sounds of a crowd cheering on a game enter, faintly. They intermingle with the sounds of a crowd in a train station.)

(The sound crescendos until it is overtaken by the whistle of a train and then a rush of train traveling closer and closer yet.)

(The swoosh of a train coming to a stop and a final whistle.)

(Silence.)

(As the lights come up, the faint sound of a single basketball dribbled on a dirt-packed court a mile away returns.)

(JEAN, *a 15 ½ year-old girl, peers out toward the sound. She is tall and skinny, but dressed in the well-worn traveling suit of a much meatier woman. She wears a hat and gloves and there is a small trunk behind her.)*

(Her skin, along with every other surface on the stage, is covered in a layer of red dust, which is stirred up occasionally by a breeze blowing through.)

(She takes off her hat and stands on tiptoe, straining to see the sounds.)

(She taps along to the rhythm of the beating basketball heart.)

JEAN. Twenty-six beats for a half-minute.
Is fifty-two beats for a minute.
Is...three-thousand one hundred twenty beats for an hour.

(She stops tapping.)

Feels like.
More than my heart will hold out.
Here.
The place where I will never be found.
Here.
This...*grave town.*

*(As she speaks, **HAUNT JOHNNY** enters from a distance. He wears a hat pulled over his eyes and a dark suit. He carries a scratched-up suitcase and a round burlap bundle. He is a handsome man of indeterminate age, but is certainly many years older than 15 ½.)*

*(He stops when he sees **JEAN** on tiptoe, still some distance away. He watches her.)*

Poor Prairie, what a grave town.

HAUNT JOHNNY. *(softly)* I saw you.

*(**JEAN** turns sharply and sees **HAUNT JOHNNY**. She pulls on her hat and sits down next to her trunk. She is suddenly conscious of the dust on her face and begins frantically wiping at it.)*

On the train.
I saw you.

(JEAN *looks down.*)

Only you were seated.

(*He looks at her legs.*)

So, I didn't see how nice and tall you are.
Seated.

(JEAN *pulls her skirt over her legs and swings them behind the trunk.*)

Train came in more'n an hour ago.
What're you doing still hanging on?

(JEAN *looks up.*)

JEAN. I might ask you the same.

(*He steps closer.*)

HAUNT JOHNNY. You might.

(*A beat.*)

You asking?

(JEAN *shrugs.*)

They got a telephone round there I been using.
And you?

JEAN. I don't think I ought to say.

HAUNT JOHNNY. Where you come from?
I saw you around Correctionville, but you looked to
have been on for some time before.
What's bringing you up here to Poor Prairie?

JEAN. I don't think I'd like to say.

HAUNT JOHNNY. Small town –
I'll find you out sooner, not later.

(*A beat.*)

Whose suit you sporting?

JEAN. Mine now.

HAUNT JOHNNY. Woman who wore it out was a lot more woman than you.

Not as nice and tall, though.

Not many women are.

(*JEAN slumps.*)

You ever heard of Babe Dublin?

Babe's Ballers?

JEAN. Sure.

HAUNT JOHNNY. She's an old friend of mine.

Haven't let myself think on her in some time.

But I must say, you are bending my mind that way again.

JEAN. Don't believe it.

HAUNT JOHNNY. It's true.

You've got her legs, the way the backs bulge out, squareish.

(*JEAN puts her hands to the back of her calves, horrified.*)

JEAN. I meant: I don't believe you're friends with her.

Or, I don't believe she'd be friends with *you*.

HAUNT JOHNNY. I lent a hand in the founding of the Ballers.

See, Poor Prairie's her hometown, too.

Her people used to live…

(**HAUNT JOHNNY** *points out at the horizon.*)

There.

JEAN. There?

(*He looks at her.*)

HAUNT JOHNNY. To your left.

JEAN. There.

Bet she never comes back.

HAUNT JOHNNY. There?

No.

JEAN. Smart. Leave here and never look back.

HAUNT JOHNNY. Fresh arrived and directly spitting to leave.

JEAN. Would that I could.

But this is my grave town.

HAUNT JOHNNY. *(laughing)* You sound like you come up here to get married.

JEAN. Something like.

HAUNT JOHNNY. What's *something like* marriage?

JEAN. You look the sort to know.

(**HAUNT JOHNNY** *crouches down to look under her hat at her face. He leans in.*)

HAUNT JOHNNY. Just a kid and already so grim.

Not like me.

I got a last best option.

(**JEAN** *snaps.*)

JEAN. What are you doing up here?

No men in Poor Prairie.

Said the conductor.

HAUNT JOHNNY. Dusty land these days.

Drove the fathers Downstate.

But! I am fresh off an education.

JEAN. You are too old to be newly schooled.

HAUNT JOHNNY. I took the long way.

JEAN. A long way that ends *here?*

HAUNT JOHNNY. Hometown.

I expect to find work here in a way I've got no right to expect from any other place.

But more than that there's –

You'll keep this close?

JEAN. Or else?

HAUNT JOHNNY. You'll have betrayed me.

I never spoke this aloud before.

(**JEAN** *looks at him for a beat.*)

JEAN. Okay.

HAUNT JOHNNY. I also come back for…

There's the sunsets.

JEAN. The sun sets everywhere.

HAUNT JOHNNY. Not like it do on that field over.

Right there, next to the school.

JEAN. There?

(**HAUNT JOHNNY** *looks at her.*)

HAUNT JOHNNY. To your left.

Stand out in that field after the school day in winter – not a tree in sight to break the view – and watch the world set fire for fifteen blazing minutes.

You'll *smell* it in Poor Prairie.

JEAN. The sun?

HAUNT JOHNNY. Now you see why I've never told a soul.

(**JEAN** *studies him.*)

JEAN. What does the sun smell like?

HAUNT JOHNNY. Like whiskey flavor pipe smoke and cloves and orange peel and snow.

The sunset smells like heat and ice in Poor Prairie and I haven't been able to smell it anywhere else.

(*He takes another step closer.*)

This town'll work on you that way.

(*He sits down next to her.*)

You'll be tied into Poor Prairie before you can say "help".

(*They sit for a moment, eyes locked.* **JEAN** *breaks away.*)

JEAN. What's that one with the pounding coming from out behind?

Twenty-six beats for a half minute.

Looks like a barn.

HAUNT JOHNNY. There?

That's a barn.

JEAN. Oh.

HAUNT JOHNNY. That's a mile away.

JEAN. Never would guess.

HAUNT JOHNNY. It's the flatness.

(He scoots next to her.)

And that one there –

JEAN. There?

HAUNT JOHNNY. There

(He reaches out slowly, as if petting a strange dog, and takes her gloved hand.)

(She blinks wildly, but does not look at him as he moves her hand to the left.)

There, to the left.

Is the farm where I grew up.

JEAN. I see.

(Slowly, **HAUNT JOHNNY** *peels off her glove.* **JEAN** *does not look at him.)*

HAUNT JOHNNY. What's your name?

*(***HAUNT JOHNNY** *inspects her hand, holding it out, stroking her fingers, pulling her thumb and pinky apart.)*

*(***JEAN** *closes her eyes.)*

JEAN. Uh.

HAUNT JOHNNY. Or you don't like to say.

JEAN. Jean.

HAUNT JOHNNY. Jean, you have hard hands.

*(***JEAN** *opens her eyes.)*

JEAN. They didn't used to be.

(He looks closer.)

HAUNT JOHNNY. Hands get harder with the times.

(He measures his own outspread hand against hers.)

JEAN. What's your name?

HAUNT JOHNNY. Johnny.

But they call me Haunt Johnny ever since I was small over there.

JEAN. Haunt Johnny?

(He nods.)

Because you are like to be a ghost.

I will blink.

And you will never have been here.

HAUNT JOHNNY. But still you would not tell a soul about the sun smell?

Even if I were to be a ghost?

*(***JEAN*** shakes her head.)*

Good girl.

(She looks down at his bundle.)

JEAN. It's an odd shape bundle.

HAUNT JOHNNY. I need something particular to keep my soul in.

JEAN. Can I see?

HAUNT JOHNNY. No.

Better you touch.

*(***HAUNT JOHNNY*** removes her other glove.)*

(He picks up the bundle, balances it between his knees, and leads her hands down inside the burlap.)

HAUNT JOHNNY. You got the feel for it?

JEAN. Is it a –

HAUNT JOHNNY. It is.

You play?

(She shakes her head.)

Never?

JEAN. They dropped the team in Brighton when I was nine.

HAUNT JOHNNY. Shame.

Being as nice and tall as you are.

(Suddenly, the sound of a sputtering car engine.)

(JEAN *springs up, jumps away from* **HAUNT JOHNNY**, *and attempts to put her gloves back on.*)

JEAN. God help me.

(*In one smooth motion,* **HAUNT JOHNNY** *sweeps up his bundle and suitcase and is gone.*)

(*When* **JEAN** *finishes putting on her gloves, she looks up to where he had been.*)

(*As she is looking at this spot,* **ALMEDA** *enters, running, from the opposite direction. She is a muscular 14 year-old and, though not small, is not as tall as* **JEAN**. **ALMEDA** *is barefoot, wears overalls, and is covered in dust and sweat; her hair is tangled and she chews bubblegum.*)

ALMEDA. Cousin Jean?

JEAN. Oh, you must be –

(**JEAN** *offers her hand.* **ALMEDA** *circles her like an animal instead.*)

Almeda.

ALMEDA. Listen to you: Almeda.

Al's trouble enough.

You're looking the lady.

And they told me you were fifteen.

JEAN. And a half.

Sixteen in five months.

ALMEDA. Well, fifteen *and a half* sure don't look like you around here.

JEAN. The train's been in for more than an hour, I thought Uncle Malcolm –

ALMEDA. Left word for me, come to find out.

But I been out, so.

JEAN. Well, I have been waiting.

It was not a short trip.

ALMEDA. Do you look like this always?

(**JEAN** *straightens the suit.*)

JEAN. It's a *traveling* suit.

Only when I travel.

(**ALMEDA** *kicks the trunk.*)

ALMEDA. You got things don't look like that?

JEAN. Everything else.

It's my mother's suit.

Remember her by.

ALMEDA. So now you'll be after my ma's things, I s'pose.

JEAN. That's quite the hello.

ALMEDA. Aw, save the speech.

She ain't had nothing nice since I was still in swaddlers.

JEAN. That's some time ago now.

You must be –

ALMEDA. Fourteen.

(*A beat.*)

JEAN. Didn't know we were so close.

ALMEDA. Well, don't forget it now.

And don't forget this:

I don't need no mother.

JEAN. Is that so?

ALMEDA. Before my ma passed, she told me:

"Al, remember me for always."

And that's the last time anybody told me what to do and I sure ain't sorry for that fact.

JEAN. Oh, no?

ALMEDA. All my ma ever did is hold me back.

I been needing to run wild *for years.*

Haven't washed my hair since the burial.

JEAN. That recently?

ALMEDA. (*intended to provoke*) Mothers are unneedful, no-fun, miserable bitches.

(*A beat.*)

You ain't gonna dispute.

JEAN. Certainly not.

Do you think I *asked* my mother to send me away?

ALMEDA. So, we agree that neither of us wants you here.

JEAN. Sure.

ALMEDA. Okay, then. We're set.

JEAN. If you mind me, we'll be fine.

ALMEDA. What's that mean?

JEAN. Meaning, *Almeda:*

I am not your mother and I did not give you life, but you will mind me – or I'll make you wish yourself dead.

ALMEDA. You don't say.

JEAN. I just did.

Now get my trunk.

It was not a short trip.

And I have been waiting.

And I would like to be in bed by dark.

ALMEDA. Uh-huh.

JEAN. Yes?

ALMEDA. Yes.

(**ALMEDA** *moves to the trunk and begins to wheel it off.*)

(**JEAN** *picks up her suitcase, smug.*)

(**ALMEDA** *stops, looks at* **JEAN**, *calculatedly.*)

Oh, I'll just need to make a short stop on the way.

JEAN. In bed by dark.

(**JEAN** *exits with her suitcase.* **ALMEDA** *watches her go. The sound of a rhythmic pounding of hard-packed dirt begins…*)

ALMEDA. Uh-huh.

(*Lights shift.*)

Two

(In darkness, a rhythmic pounding against hard-packed dirt.)

(A lantern up on **INEZ**, *a womanly 17 year-old of average height [like* **ALMEDA**, *she is shorter than* **JEAN***]. She wears a loose-fitting light-colored dress and dark shoes; she pounds the hard ground with a shovel.)*

(She pauses for a moment to wipe her sweaty, dusty forehead.)

ALMEDA. Inez!

(A beat. Muffled coughing offstage.)

INEZ. *(a hiss) Over here.*

*(***ALMEDA*** *enters.* **INEZ** *scoops up some broken-up earth with the shovel.)*

ALMEDA. Inez, I come special!

*(***ALMEDA*** *pats the pocket of her overall bib as* **INEZ** *removes a jug from the ground.)*

INEZ. C'mon.

*(***ALMEDA*** *runs to* **INEZ** *who playfights with her a little.)*

You loud mouth –

Hazel Shoots'll hear you all the way to Humboldt.

ALMEDA. Hazel the Has-Been and her shriveled-up old basketball.

INEZ. It was big of her to leave it behind for us, Al.

(muffled coughing offstage)

ALMEDA. You got your brothers and sisters to bed?

INEZ. And dug us up some swill.

We got the run of the plains tonight, girly.

JEAN. *(offstage)* Almeda!

ALMEDA. Urgh, I told her to stay put!

Jean!

INEZ. Who's the lady?

(JEAN *enters, tottering in her heels.*)

JEAN. I need water.

ALMEDA. You'll see in day, it's just the suit.

JEAN. *(coughing)* Road was all dust.

ALMEDA. Inez is seventeen.

(INEZ *hands* JEAN *the jug.*)

JEAN. Thank you!

(JEAN *takes a huge gulp of the jug.*)

ALMEDA. And 5, 4, 3 –

(JEAN *spits out a mouthful of liquid.*)

INEZ. She's quicker'n you counted on.

(JEAN *makes retching sounds.*)

JEAN. Not water.

INEZ. Corn whiskey.

JEAN. *(low)* You will repent this.

INEZ. Nice and tall.
Where she come from?

ALMEDA. Back East.

INEZ. Why's she here?

(ALMEDA *hands* INEZ *the jug.*)

ALMEDA. Meant to hold me and the farm down.

INEZ. Doesn't sum up.
Why would your Pa take on another mouth now?
I don't think this is about you.

(JEAN *steps away.* INEZ *watches her.*)

There's more to this story than we know.

ALMEDA. I've come to be too much to handle, I heard
Puppy Dibbit's mother say.

INEZ. Mrs. Dibbit's got a mind to make a name for herself.
She went Downstate last week.

ALMEDA. The capitol?

INEZ. For a committee.

ALMEDA. What's the committee?

INEZ. On play.

ALMEDA. Play?

What's that mean?

JEAN. I know what that means.

(**ALMEDA** *turns.*)

ALMEDA. You been here two hours and *you know what that means?*

JEAN. Take me to the house and I'll tell.

(**ALMEDA** *moves as if to grab* **JEAN**'s *hair.*)

ALMEDA. That's it, I'mma lock you in your luggage.

INEZ. You couldn't.

She wouldn't fit.

ALMEDA. Then I got rope in the car.

INEZ. Ooooh, that's good.

ALMEDA. She thinks she'll boss me down?

Then I'll tie up her mouth for a while.

(**ALMEDA** *exits.*)

JEAN. I won't live like this.

INEZ. She's an acquired taste.

Like corn whiskey.

(**INEZ** *holds up the jug, playfully.*)

JEAN. Just point me in the right direction.

INEZ. Why don't you tell me about this committee on play?

(**JEAN** *lunges for the shovel, swinging the jug at* **INEZ**.)

JEAN. I'll take the lantern and I'll find another driver.

(**INEZ** *reaches out for her.*)

INEZ. You'll be sorry if you run off, Jean.

You don't want to get into the cars that'll come for you.

JEAN. *(yelling)* Help!

(**INEZ** *lunges for her and covers her mouth, removing the shovel and jug from* **JEAN***'s hands.*)

INEZ. Don't do this now.

(**JEAN** *screams, muffled.*)

We can have the run of the plains, long as we keep it quiet.

(**JEAN** *screams again, muffled.*)

At least wait to make a run for it til you'll have a real chance of getting away.

(**JEAN** *quiets.*)

You understand?

(**JEAN** *nods.* **INEZ** *eases her down to the ground and holds the back of* **JEAN***'s head, lifting the jug up to* **JEAN***'s lips.*)

(**JEAN** *shakes her head.*)

You'll feel better.

(**INEZ** *tips her head back, gently, and* **JEAN** *takes a drink.* **JEAN** *slumps down as* **INEZ** *sits next to her.*)

(*A beat.*)

You see?

JEAN. The committee on play is the former First Lady's pet project.

(**INEZ** *looks at her.*)

INEZ. Mrs. Hoover?

JEAN. She started speaking on it Back East years ago.
This place is such a grave town.

INEZ. So, what's it mean: Play?

JEAN. Kind of thing that ends up in physicians warning about overexertion and impediments to childbearing.

INEZ. Sport?

JEAN. *Girls'* sport.

INEZ. Impediments to childbearing!

That'd be a blessing.

My ma played point and she's still got six plus me.

JEAN. It's inappropriate, they say.

INEZ. Y'know, I'd never even heard that word before Mrs. Dibbit chaperoned me and Puppy and Hazel Shoots to the tournament Downstate three years back. Directly after, she had a mile-long list of what Puppy wasn't supposed to do.

JEAN. You *played*? In a tournament?

INEZ. Did my best.

But Hazel was the star.

When she graduated that year, we lost steam.

What about you?

JEAN. Me?

(**ALMEDA** *enters, carrying a coil of rope. She stops, seeing* **INEZ** *and* **JEAN** *sitting together.*)

INEZ. You play?

You got the height for it.

ALMEDA. WHAT are you doing, chumming with her?

INEZ. Al, Jean's sorry she made a fuss.

Why don't you take her home and let her get some sleep?

ALMEDA. It's not *her* home.

She ain't even blood to my pa.

My dead mother's sister's daughter.

INEZ. And here I thought I'd already put all the babies to bed.

ALMEDA. Inez, I come here special.

With a new dollar.

INEZ. Lemme see.

ALMEDA. You come close.

Away from her.

(**INEZ** *stands and walks over to* **ALMEDA** *who takes two steps away.* **INEZ** *closes the gap.* **ALMEDA** *fishes a dollar coin from out of the front of her overalls.*)

INEZ. Would you look at that.

JEAN. Where'd you get a dollar?

INEZ. Al, it's beautiful.

ALMEDA. Can we sum it up?

INEZ. Of course.

> (**ALMEDA** *kisses* **INEZ** *on the cheek as she gives her the coin.*)

> (**INEZ** *picks up the shovel and runs over to the hole. She scoops out a little more dirt and removes a filthy-looking doll. She pulls up the doll's dress and reaches inside her belly to pull out a jar.* **INEZ** *unscrews the jar and pours out coins into her hand. She counts them back into the jar.*)

> (*She pulls out a tightly rolled-up scrap of brown paper and a small pencil. She writes on the paper.*)

INEZ. Two dollars and six cents.

ALMEDA. A new bladder costs – ?

INEZ. Three dollars and fifteen cents, plus sixteen cents postage and special delivery fee.

Sum that up –

> (**INEZ** *scratches for a second.*)

JEAN. You need another dollar and a quarter.

> (**INEZ** *looks up at* **ALMEDA**.)

INEZ. Quicker'n I can count.

JEAN. What're you buying a bladder for?

ALMEDA. Doesn't concern you.

INEZ. Factor in shipping time...

ALMEDA. Harvest's over.

INEZ. I know that.

ALMEDA. Means school's starting back for the winter in four days.

First game's in twelve.

INEZ. I *know* that.

JEAN. A bladder –

ALMEDA. Inez, I gotta go Downstate this year.

JEAN. – for a basketball?

ALMEDA. Yes, of course.

    Of course we're talking about a basketball.

JEAN. I'm only asking because…

ALMEDA. Hazel Shoots didn't get Downstate until her senior year.

    On account of she could only practice at practice times.

    Cuz you were all sharing that one no-good, hobble-bounce ball.

INEZ. I remember, Al.

ALMEDA. I *need* my own basketball now.

    I gotta be able to practice day and night to have a real shot.

INEZ. I'll help any way I can.

JEAN. The man I met at the depot had one.

    From the feel of it, brand new.

    *(**ALMEDA** and **INEZ** look at her.)*

    (A long beat.)

ALMEDA. From the *feel* of it?

    What do you know about the *feel* of a basketball?

JEAN. Nothing. Just that –

    The leather felt like…pebbled.

    Like when I used to have new shoes in the fall.

INEZ. Hazel's ball's been fish-slippery for years.

    (A beat.)

    What were the laces like?

JEAN. I don't know

    Raised?

ALMEDA. How high?

    *(**JEAN** shows with her thumb and forefinger. **INEZ** raises the lantern ever so slightly to look.)*

ALMEDA. I don't believe it.

> She's dressing up the truth worse than Lurlene Lonestead.

INEZ. Lurlene's lies are as long as her legs.

> Al, I don't think that's what this is.

ALMEDA. Then what's she doing talking to strange men at the depot, huh?

INEZ. And getting a feel of their luggage?

> *(INEZ looks at JEAN.)*

> More to this story than we know.

> Question is: who's the man with a brand-new basketball?

> *(INEZ and ALMEDA look back at JEAN.)*

JEAN. Take me home and I'll tell.

ALMEDA. Not *your* home!

INEZ. You want that basketball, Al? Take her home.

> *(The sound of apples dropping into a bucket begins...)*

ALMEDA. Uh-huh.

> *(Lights shift.)*

> *(In the transition,* **JEAN** *grabs* **ALMEDA** *and holds her down to brush her hair, roughly.)*

Three

*(Lights up on **LURLENE**, 16, standing onstage with a cigarette and a photograph. She wears a floral dress and flat shoes and is taller than even **JEAN**. A shriveled-up old graying basketball lies next to her.)*

(As she talks, she plays around with the unlit cigarette, mimicking glamour poses.)

LURLENE. She finally gave it to me, Puppy. After three solid years of humbling myself to my knees, donchaknow, Inez finally put it into my hands. And I been looking at Hazel Shoots' Downstate Tournament Royalty photograph like my eyes were gumstuck to it ever since. For the last six days, I have been painting my nails, bathing, and relieving myself with this image, that's how devoted I've been to Hazel's likeness.

And the thing I see is: Hazel Shoots was given *a tiara*. Hazel Shoots was *crowned* Queen of the Tournament. Never mind that she only made it out over to Humboldt to marry a player from the Humboldt boys' team, because she got a *tiara*. Well, this leads me to the other bit I noticed in my study of Hazel Shoots' features, which is:

She isn't no better looking than me.

For one, she has an inferior Cupid's bow. And still! She was given a tiara. Only think on what could've happened to me if I'da been old enough to go Downstate with my superior Cupid's bow three years back. It was then I pulled out my old copy of *The Red Book* – you know the one with the photo of the Babe's Ballers inside. (I don't spend time on that picture, Babe Dublin looks like a sweaty wrestler in a wig). No, I flip through the close-ups of starlets and socialites in satin and, again, do you know what I found?

There are plenty of starlets and socialites who don't look all that much better than Hazel Shoots, meaning that there are plenty who don't look half as good as

me. So now I'm thinking to myself, could be I should
be in satin. To do that, I'd need to leave Poor Prairie.
They're all wearing white in those photos and you
know as well as me it's near unthinkable to keep white
bleached and clean here. But what if I could leave
Poor Prairie? (And not for trouble of the nine-month
variety neither. Lord knows the girls who get sent away
for a little less than a year…those girls certainly ain't
wearing white.) No, I gotta go somewhere where I
could wear nail paint everyday.

And donchaknow it was with that thought in my head
that I answered the door this morning and saw Cyril
Cosgrove standing there with his hat in his hand.
I said: "Cyril, I don't mean to bust up your heart – I
never wanted it to end this way – but I come to see that
I am a better looker than not only former Tournament
Queen Hazel Shoots," – I showed him the photograph
at that point, since I had it, like I been saying, handy.
"But also a good number of the starlets and socialites
in *The Red Book*, which leads me to say that I am not
long for Poor Prairie. Which leads me to say that we
are not long for our love. Please, go quietly, I don't
think I could survive a scene!"

*(PUPPY enters, carrying a basket of apples. PUPPY is 18
years old, but might pass for 12. She is tiny and wears
a neat, girlish dress; her clothing is of significantly better
quality than anyone else's.)*

PUPPY. I don't want to disappoint, but.

This was everything I could reach from the top rung.

LURLENE. And with that, I lit up the cigarette I been
holding and took a long drag –

(LURLENE mimes the action.)

PUPPY. I don't want to disappoint, so.

I got up onto my tippy toes.

LURLENE. – and blew the smoke in his face like in a
photograph from *The Red Book* and said again:
"Just go, I don't think I could survive a scene!"

(A beat.)

PUPPY. So, what then?

(LURLENE turns her head, but the rest of her body remains frozen in the pose.)

What'd *he* say, Lurlene?

(LURLENE unfreezes from the pose, slumps.)

LURLENE. He, uh.

He said nothing.

He waved away the smoke and turned and walked back to his pa's truck and drove away.

PUPPY. He did?

LURLENE. Turns out he'd come to tell me he was going away to St. John's seminary on scholarship.

I didn't ever expect *Cyril* to bust it up with *me.*

PUPPY. Better he become a priest, Lurlene.

I would've missed you too much if you'd gone and married Cyril.

LURLENE. He did show a restraint when it came to my charms that is, in my experience, uncustomary to the male sex.

(LURLENE looks at the basket of apples.)

This isn't even half a bushel.

PUPPY. It's everything I could reach.

I'm small.

LURLENE. I'm meant to bake 20 pies.

I told you I would tell you the story in return.

Now I've told the story and I can't take it back but you haven't held up your end.

PUPPY. I have prayed every night since I was eight years old for a growth spurt.

That's ten years of unanswered prayers, Lurlene.

LURLENE. I'm likely to ruin my nails.

I've stretched this coat six days now.

PUPPY. Mother says painted girls have all-too-colorful reputations.

(She holds up a finger.)

See, I'll take the broom for this.

*(**LURLENE** grabs **PUPPY**'s finger.)*

LURLENE. A scratch?

PUPPY. The hands of ladies are the hands of babies.
No dirt, no blisters, no scars.

*(**LURLENE** picks up the deflated, graying basketball.)*

LURLENE. You're gonna get corn calluses when we start running drills again.

PUPPY. I'm not certain.

LURLENE. They don't file down, I've tried –

PUPPY. No, I mean.
I'm not certain I'll be running drills, Lurlene.
Mother's threatening to bust up basketball for me.

LURLENE. Well, don't tell Al, she'll murder you with her own two.
She thinks she's a player away from reviving the team.

PUPPY. Another element Mother frowns on now:
Al.

LURLENE. Aw, tell her to tug off.

PUPPY. She'll ship me Downstate to St. Catherine-on-the-Wheel if I cross her.

LURLENE. Why don't your ma ship *herself* Downstate it pain her so to be here?

PUPPY. Father won't let her.
Long as corn prices stay so low and farm foreclosures so high, there's good work for a lawyer in this county.

LURLENE. There ain't a lot of fun here, Pup – we can't afford to lose a drop.

(A sputtering car engine is heard distantly.)

PUPPY. I ought to be back.

LURLENE. It's Al.

PUPPY. Mother always knows.

 (The engine cuts out.)

ALMEDA. *(offstage)* Lurlene!
 Puppy!

 *(**PUPPY** looks out and waves, pained, and then tucks her head down and runs offstage.)*

LURLENE. Al, come hear the story.
 I busted up Cyril Cosgrove's heart.

 *(**ALMEDA** enters, dressed as before.)*

ALMEDA. No time.
 I'm on the scent of a basketball.

LURLENE. You're here for your turn.

 *(**LURLENE** picks up the shriveled ball.)*

ALMEDA. Don't need Hazel's hand-me-down no more.
 Now that there's a brand new ball in town.

LURLENE. Says who?

 *(**ALMEDA** looks off in the direction from which she entered.)*

ALMEDA. *(calling off)* Jean!

 (A car door opens and closes like a ball bouncing.)

LURLENE. Who?

ALMEDA. *(calling off)* Jean!

 *(**LURLENE** squints offstage.)*

LURLENE. Who's that?

ALMEDA. That's –

 *(**JEAN** enters; she wears a smart, but worn-looking dress.)*
 Jean.

JEAN. *(low)* Leave off the shrieking or you will repent.

ALMEDA. Jean, Lurlene. Lurlene, Jean.
 My cousin from Back East.

JEAN. *(civilized)* How do you do?

(JEAN and LURLENE shake hands. LURLENE is impressed by JEAN's manners.)

LURLENE. Back East?

You been to New York City?

JEAN. Yes, of course.

(ALMEDA selects an apple from the basket.)

Don't you dare spoil your supper, Almeda.

(LURLENE wipes dust off JEAN's lips with her thumb. The gesture is a bit rough.)

(ALMEDA makes a show of taking a big bite of apple as she locks eyes with JEAN.)

LURLENE. You got a good Cupid's bow.

Shiny hair, lively eyes.

(to ALMEDA:) She know she got a nice look to her?

ALMEDA. *(chewing, looking at JEAN)* What do I know what she knows?

JEAN. If you won't mind our bad manners, Lurlene: We ought to go.

LURLENE. She talks soft like in the pictures.

ALMEDA. *(to JEAN:)* But I ain't finished telling her about the brand new basketball.

LURLENE. Who's got rub enough for a new ball?

ALMEDA. This is where you come in.

JEAN. A man.

(A beat.)

(LURLENE strikes a satisfied pose.)

LURLENE. This *is* where I come in.

(ALMEDA grins, looks at JEAN.)

ALMEDA. You said his people come from over there?

(ALMEDA points. JEAN moves her hand.)

JEAN. To the left.

(The sound of a basketball bouncing on hard-packed dirt a mile away begins.)

ALMEDA. The Oddment place?

Even better.

Outskirts.

LURLENE. No witnesses.

*(**JEAN** sighs, looks back at her. **ALMEDA** plays serious.)*

JEAN. You have ten minutes.

No more.

*(**ALMEDA** nods soberly as **JEAN** turns to leave. When **JEAN** turns around, **ALMEDA** looks at **LURLENE**, grinning again.)*

ALMEDA. Uh-huh.

(Lights shift.)

Four

(The sound of a basketball bouncing on hard-packed dirt.)

(A glowing light up on **HAUNT JOHNNY**, *dribbling a pristine, oxblood-colored basketball. Dust clouds swirl up as the ball hits the dirt surface. He shoots the ball up into a dinged-up metal rim.)*

(JEAN *enters, transfixed.)*

(She watches him from a distance.)

ALMEDA. *(offstage)* Jean?

(HAUNT JOHNNY *turns to look at the sound as* **JEAN** *attempts to hide.)*

HAUNT JOHNNY. Is that –
Jean?

(LURLENE *steps forward.)*

LURLENE. No, your luck.
Lurlene.

HAUNT JOHNNY. What is it I can do for you… Lurlene?

LURLENE. Better question is: What *couldn't* you do for me? *Johnny*, is it?

HAUNT JOHNNY. How'd you know that?

LURLENE. You got the look of a Johnny.

HAUNT JOHNNY. *Haunt* Johnny.
There were others around when my name stuck on.

LURLENE. Well, I expect you're one of a kind nowadays.
As such, you'll be attracting yourself some attention.

(LURLENE *steps closer.)*

HAUNT JOHNNY. What you call attention, I name trouble.

LURLENE. Call me whatever you like.

(LURLENE *takes another step in.* **HAUNT JOHNNY** *turns his head away from her.)*

HAUNT JOHNNY. Whew, that's an...unnatural scent, Lurlene.

LURLENE. Thank you.

HAUNT JOHNNY. That strike you as a compliment?

LURLENE. The trouble I go to in my toilet wouldn't be worth much if it just turned out natural.

(**HAUNT JOHNNY** *leans in to look at her closer.*)

HAUNT JOHNNY. Hold on now:
   Lurlene?

LURLENE. *(breathily)* Yes?

HAUNT JOHNNY. You the Lonestead girl?

LURLENE. Nobody's ever lone when I'm in stead.

HAUNT JOHNNY. Christ.
   Lurlene Lonestead, I can think on you as a baby.
   Used to come round for your brother.

(**LURLENE** *is taken off-guard.*)

LURLENE. *(losing her sense of purpose)* You knew Terrence?

HAUNT JOHNNY. Played ball with him.
   And Babe Dublin.

LURLENE. *Terrence* played basketball with Babe Dublin?

HAUNT JOHNNY. Used to pick up a game with her in the evenings after practice.
   There was a boys' team then.

LURLENE. I been to see the boys play in Humboldt, but here.
   Ain't been enough able-bodied for years.

HAUNT JOHNNY. Those were good times:
   We had the run of the plains.
   How the hairy hell's Terrence doing these days?

LURLENE. Oh.
   He's dead.
   Threshing accident.
   Back before the dust, when there was still work for hire.

HAUNT JOHNNY. I sure am sorry.

LURLENE. I was just a baby.

HAUNT JOHNNY. Like I said, I can think on you then.

(*A shift.*)

LURLENE. Ya know, as of this morning, I am in between admirers.

HAUNT JOHNNY. Lurlene, what're you after here?

LURLENE. A trade.

HAUNT JOHNNY. What kinda *trade*?

LURLENE. You lemme hold that basketball for a few weeks.

HAUNT JOHNNY. And?

LURLENE. I'll be grateful.

(**LURLENE** *takes a step forward,* **HAUNT JOHNNY** *steps back.*)

(**HAUNT JOHNNY** *kicks the ball up onto his palm.*)

HAUNT JOHNNY. You got the height for basketball.

(*A beat.*)

LURLENE. But?

HAUNT JOHNNY. You don't practice.

Nail paint tells me that much.

LURLENE. Maybe I'm just that good.

I got the longest pair of legs in two counties, Johnny darling.

HAUNT JOHNNY. More the shame.

All the ladies industrial leagues and the barnstormers like Babe's are playing men now.

Tall girls are in demand.

And you're putting those legs to waste.

LURLENE. I dispute:

I get good use out of 'em.

HAUNT JOHNNY. Showy and undisciplined, just like your brother.

LURLENE. You know what else I can put to good use?

Balls.

(LURLENE swipes the ball.)

HAUNT JOHNNY. It's the one I have the feel for, Lurlene. I can't give it away easy.

LURLENE. Like I said, I'd be grateful.

(LURLENE steps closer.)

How about I come by next week to return the ball –

(LURLENE shifts the ball into one hand and grabs his crotch with the other.)

And I say thank you proper?

(A beat.)

(HAUNT JOHNNY removes her hand from him with one hand and swats the ball away from her with the other. The ball is sent bouncing. LURLENE is knocked off balance; the ball rolls away.)

(JEAN steps out of hiding ever so slightly to look at the ball.)

HAUNT JOHNNY. Sloppy, Lurlene.
Protect the ball.
I don't want you coming back, you hear?

(HAUNT JOHNNY recovers the ball.)

I'll give you time with the ball often enough.

(LURLENE looks a little hopeful.)

LURLENE. Oh?

HAUNT JOHNNY. At school.

LURLENE. You'll come after me?

HAUNT JOHNNY. I'm the new teacher, Lurlene.

(HAUNT JOHNNY turns to leave.)

Good day then.

(HAUNT JOHNNY turns back.)

And tell Jean and your friend behind the silo they'll have some time with the ball, too.

(HAUNT JOHNNY exits.)

(ALMEDA slinks out of her hiding place.)

LURLENE. Al, you owe me major!

ALMEDA. For what?

You didn't get me my brand new basketball!

LURLENE. My nail paint.

Six days of preservation to waste.

ALMEDA. No sense wishing on passing marks now, huh?

(JEAN steps out.)

JEAN. Come now.

(In the distance, the sound of running footsteps on hard-packed dirt and school desks being dragged into place begins…)

ALMEDA. Lurlene copped herself a tickle on *the new teacher!* AND he pushed her away!

LURLENE. Go hang yourself, Al.

JEAN. We ought to get away from here.

ALMEDA. And get myself that goddamn ball.

(They exit, **JEAN** *looking back at* **HAUNT JOHNNY**'s *offstage house one last time as she goes.)*

(Lights shift.)

(In the transition, **ALMEDA** *attempts to dribble Hazel's deflated old ball.)*

Five

(Running footsteps grow closer as:)

(Lights come up on **INEZ**, **LURLENE**, **ALMEDA**, *and* **PUPPY** *in a classroom.)*

*(***HAUNT JOHNNY**, *Hazel's basketball under his arm, consults scribbled notes.)*

HAUNT JOHNNY. Last season, Babe's Ballers played a twenty-five game stretch Out West, winning 88% of their scheduled games.

*(***ALMEDA** *raises her hand.)*

Yes?

ALMEDA. It's true you had a hand in the founding of the Ballers?

That you're a close personal friend of the greatest lady ball player of all time?

HAUNT JOHNNY. This is an arithmetic lesson, – ?

ALMEDA. Name's Al.

HAUNT JOHNNY. This is an arithmetic lesson, *Al.*

ALMEDA. Sure, but I just wanna know:

You're gonna give me that brand new basketball?

Then you'll coach us, right?

First game's next week.

HAUNT JOHNNY. How many games did the Ballers win?

*(***HAUNT JOHNNY** *throws the ball at* **INEZ**, *hard.)*

INEZ. I like to follow my work with a pencil.

HAUNT JOHNNY. Well, that skirts the point of learning to think on your feet.

Inez, right?

Pass the ball.

*(***ALMEDA** *claps and signals that she's open.)*

ALMEDA. I got this.

*(***INEZ** *passes* **ALMEDA** *the ball.)*

LURLENE. *(to* **JOHNNY,** *uncrossing her legs)* And here I was, *wide open,* ready to receive a pass.

*(***JEAN*** *enters quietly. She doesn't look entirely well.* **ALMEDA** *starts dribbling.)*

HAUNT JOHNNY. Al?

You got the answer?

ALMEDA. No, the ball.

HAUNT JOHNNY. Do the arithmetic.

ALMEDA. What do I need arithmetic for when I got the ball?

HAUNT JOHNNY. Because your head ought to be quick as your hands.

*(***ALMEDA*** *stops dribbling.)*

ALMEDA. Sounds like the kinda thing a coach would say.

HAUNT JOHNNY. Don't be a ball hog –

Pass the ball, Al.

*(***HAUNT JOHNNY*** *looks at* **JEAN,** *who is now standing in such a location as to be the only logical person for* **ALMEDA** *to pass to.* **JEAN,** *still looking at* **JOHNNY,** *puts her hands up to indicate that she's open, then turns to look at* **ALMEDA.***)*

88% of 25. Al, do the arithmetic or pass the ball.

*(***ALMEDA*** *looks at* **JEAN** *and then looks away and passes the ball to* **HAUNT JOHNNY.** **HAUNT JOHNNY** *passes the ball to* **JEAN.***)*

JEAN. It's 22.

Sir.

*(***HAUNT JOHNNY*** *looks back at his notes.)*

HAUNT JOHNNY. That's correct.

Late.

But correct.

*(***JEAN*** *nods and passes the ball back as* **HAUNT JOHNNY** *returns to his scrawled notes.)*

HAUNT JOHNNY. Next.

If the home team is up at half, 26-17 and the visitors will score half the home team's halftime total in the third quarter –

(**PUPPY** *raises her hand.*)

PUPPY. Mr. Oddment, sir.

HAUNT JOHNNY. Haunt Johnny will do, –?

PUPPY. Puppy, sir.

HAUNT JOHNNY. How many baskets do the home team have to make in the third quarter to maintain their lead, Puppy?

(**HAUNT JOHNNY** *passes* **PUPPY** *the ball.*)

PUPPY. I don't want to disappoint, sir.

I'm only wondering:

May we do proper arithmetic?

HAUNT JOHNNY. I'm asking you for sums.

Pass the ball if you can't do the work.

PUPPY. It's just.

HAUNT JOHNNY. What's the trouble?

PUPPY. I don't think scorekeeping is likely to stay.

(**PUPPY** *starts to pass the ball to* **LURLENE,** *but* **HAUNT JOHNNY** *intercepts it.*)

HAUNT JOHNNY. And how exactly would that work?

Who would determine a winner in a basketball game when nobody's counting?

PUPPY. I think that would be the point.

There would be no winners.

HAUNT JOHNNY. And where's the sport in that?

Babe's Ballers wins by a landslide, but no one knows who to pay the proceeds to at the end of the night because nobody counted?

PUPPY. Well, sir, in that case.

Nobody would be paid.

ALMEDA. But they won the games fair and square.

PUPPY. It's called "play" for a reason.

And the notion of professionals is unnatural.

Who can trust an adult who plays at a child's game all day?

INEZ. You sound like your mother.

PUPPY. As she remembers, Mr. Oddment, you vagabonded your way out of town.

When you weren't but Lurlene's age.

HAUNT JOHNNY. Puppy.

Your father is –

PUPPY. Edmund Dibbit.

HAUNT JOHNNY. Attorney at law.

Only man making money when the price of corn freefalls, they say.

PUPPY. That's nothing to do with me.

LURLENE. He used to be the sponsor for the basketball team.

Before Mrs. Dibbit went Downstate for the tournament and saw St. Catherine-on-the-Wheel.

INEZ. The Wellesley of the prairie.

LURLENE. They wear white gloves at afternoon tea.

ALMEDA. Mrs. Dibbit's got a whole list of what ladies do and don't do from some Committee.

PUPPY. Mother is Poor Prairie's representative to the state assembly hosting the Committee on Play.

HAUNT JOHNNY. She's been listening to Mrs. Hoover and her leading society ladies?

PUPPY. All I know is it would save me trouble to not come home smelling of basketball leather.

If we could only do proper arithmetic.

(A beat.)

HAUNT JOHNNY. In that event:

You may confirm to your mother that I made my way out of town hustling pick-up games.

And then I got learning late.

PUPPY. Where?

INEZ. Puppy!

A teacher's college.

(*to* **HAUNT JOHNNY**:) Right?

HAUNT JOHNNY. The South.

(*A beat.*)

Where I learned at least enough to know when I'm not wanted.

No more basketball.

(**HAUNT JOHNNY** *picks up the ball and walks it over to its burlap covering in the corner. He walks back to the girls.*)

No more basketball.

(*He looks down at his scribbled notes.*)

So, then.

Two ladies are, eh.

…needlepointing?

(**PUPPY** *nods.*)

…at a rate of ten, uh, samplers? per fifteen minutes.

(**ALMEDA** *raises her hand.*)

Al, you got this?

ALMEDA. What do you mean by "no more basketball"?

HAUNT JOHNNY. I told you: I understand basketball isn't wanted around here.

(**ALMEDA** *raises her hand and begins speaking immediately.*)

ALMEDA. But the first game of the season is next week.

I'll be needing the brand new basketball.

And you.

INEZ. A coach chaperone – adult, non-student – needs to be present at competition.

HAUNT JOHNNY. You know that to the letter.

INEZ. We looked into making our own way without Miss Hurt last season –

ALMEDA. After their seventh loss.

HAUNT JOHNNY. That's not an acceptable record.
  (looking at **PUPPY***:)* If we're keeping score.

ALMEDA. No, it ain't.
  My first eligible season, I gotta make it Downstate.

LURLENE. I need a shot at tourney royalty.

ALMEDA. Will you be our coach?
  Don't have to be more'n your scribble on a piece of paper.
  I know plenty of the game myself.

  (A beat.)

HAUNT JOHNNY. No.

ALMEDA. And why not?

HAUNT JOHNNY. First thing, I'm gonna put my name on something, I'm gonna mean it.
  Second, I don't see that you have a team, Al.

ALMEDA. I got me at shooting guard.

HAUNT JOHNNY. You picture yourself the star?

ALMEDA. I want it worse than anybody.
  As bad as Babe Dublin.

HAUNT JOHNNY. That's quite a statement.

ALMEDA. And we got Inez.
  She'll do as I say to keep me quiet.
  She's small forward.

  *(***INEZ*** nods.)*

LURLENE. And I got the height for center.

HAUNT JOHNNY. Three isn't a team.
  You got a point guard?

  *(***LURLENE, ALMEDA,*** and **INEZ*** encircle* **PUPPY.***)*

ALMEDA. *Puppy?*

PUPPY. I don't want to disappoint, but.
  I can't.

HAUNT JOHNNY. Then you don't have a team, Al.

PUPPY. Don't be sore.

I just can't cross her.

ALMEDA. It's us or her.

INEZ. Al's right in her way, dear.

LURLENE. You might as well be shipped off to St. Catherine-on-the-Wheel now if you're not gonna help.

PUPPY. Lurlene, that's not fair.

I don't want to go away, every friend I have in the world is in this room.

I just don't want to disappoint anyone.

ALMEDA. You're never a disappointment when you play, Puppy.

Fastest guard around.

(**PUPPY** *looks around.*)

PUPPY. Not sure how I'd get out of the house.

LURLENE. Don't worry.

I got pointers for you.

PUPPY. *(resignation)* I don't want to disappoint anyone.

(**ALMEDA** *gives* **PUPPY** *a playful noogie as* **LURLENE** *and* **INEZ** *hug her.*)

HAUNT JOHNNY. But that's only four.

One more.

Jean?

ALMEDA. We don't need Jean.

Lurlene can fudge on the papers for Inez's little sister.

HAUNT JOHNNY. You need a strong forward.

If you want me, you need Jean.

(**HAUNT JOHNNY** *and* **JEAN** *lock eyes.*)

Nice and tall.

Got the hands for it.

Legs too.

LURLENE. *(sarcastic)* Don't forget her good Cupid's bow.

JEAN. I'm not sure my Uncle Malcolm will be able to spare me.

I'm here to hold down the house.

INEZ. Don't worry.

    I got pointers for you.

JEAN. I've never played.

INEZ. That's what practices are for.

    *(**JEAN** looks at **HAUNT JOHNNY**.)*

JEAN. A last best option?

    *(**HAUNT JOHNNY** pulls out the burlap sack.)*

INEZ. Is that – ?

    (He begins to pull the ball out of the burlap sack.)

ALMEDA. The *brand new basketball.*

HAUNT JOHNNY. *(to* **JEAN***:)*

    This is the one I've got the feel for…

    You'll keep this close?

JEAN. Yes.

    *(He passes **JEAN** the ball. She looks at her outspread hand on the leather.)*

    I'll play.

HAUNT JOHNNY. Then you have a coach.

INEZ. And we have a basketball team.

HAUNT JOHNNY. I think you might recess for ten minutes before practice.

ALMEDA. Now lemme hold that brand new ball.

    *(**ALMEDA** swipes the ball from **JEAN** as she exits with **PUPPY**, **INEZ** and **LURLENE**. Before she leaves, she stops to smell it.)*

    GodDAMN, that's nice!

HAUNT JOHNNY. Jean, a word.

    *(**JEAN** hangs back.)*

JEAN. I won't be late again, I was just a bit…unwell.

HAUNT JOHNNY. As long as we're understood.

    *(He looks down and **JEAN** starts to exit, then turns back.)*

JEAN. Each basket's worth two points?

HAUNT JOHNNY. We'll study over all that soon.

JEAN. Sure, but:

It's three.

HAUNT JOHNNY. Three?

JEAN. Baskets.

Worth two points each or two worth two and one worth one.

Would allow the home team to maintain a lead after the third quarter.

32-30 or 31-30.

*(**HAUNT JOHNNY** glances at his notes.)*

HAUNT JOHNNY. Good hands.

Good legs.

And a great head.

*(**JEAN** looks at her feet.)*

JEAN. Thank you.

HAUNT JOHNNY. The makings of a great shooting guard.

*(**JEAN** looks at him.)*

JEAN. Oh.

But Almeda –

HAUNT JOHNNY. Go out and play, Jean.

*(**JEAN** nods and dribbling is heard offstage.)*

(Lights shift.)

*(In the transition light, a passing drill. Nearing the end of the drill, **JEAN** signals to **ALMEDA** that she is open and **ALMEDA** refuses to pass the ball as before.)*

Six

(**ALMEDA** *dribbles as* **INEZ** *guards her.*)

ALMEDA. When I woke up, she was holding my head down
to the mattress.
Trying to wash my face!

INEZ. She's likely just trying to keep her place.

(**ALMEDA** *throws an elbow.*)

That's a foul, Al.

ALMEDA. The foul is:
She's only doing it to sweeten up my pa.
Why can't she keep me out of it?

(**JEAN** *enters.*)

JEAN. Almeda, I've been calling for you.

ALMEDA. Stiff off.
I'm practicing.

JEAN. I want to practice, too.
I need to learn to throw frees.

(**INEZ** *and* **ALMEDA** *laugh.*)

ALMEDA. THROW FREES?!?

INEZ. She's new to ballbasket.

ALMEDA. She stinks as bad as my old All-Stars.

INEZ. It's true.
But if you think about it –
That hurts you worse than it hurts her.

(*A beat.*)

ALMEDA. Fine.
Which is your good hand?

JEAN. Both.
Depends.

ALMEDA. But when you write, which looks shaky like you
been drinking gin all day?

JEAN. Neither.

ALMEDA. Nobody has both hands good.

INEZ. No, I've heard – some people do.

ALMEDA. Then pick a hand.

(JEAN *does.*)

No, you don't hold it flat in the palm of your hand!

(INEZ *takes the ball and puts it in* JEAN*'s hand.*)

INEZ. Balance the ball on your fingertips.

(INEZ *stands behind her and moves her into position.*)

Then you angle the shooting hand and steady the ball with the other.

ALMEDA. What do you need to touch her for?

INEZ. And release it all together.

(JEAN *shoots;* INEZ *rebounds.*)

ALMEDA. Hobble arm.

INEZ. Al, why don't you go away and let us practice?

JEAN. No, Almeda: Stay.

I need to practice against you.

ALMEDA. Ha.

JEAN. If I'm going to be a better shooting guard than you.

I need to practice against you.

(ALMEDA *grabs the ball;* JEAN *does not let go.*)

INEZ. That's a held ball.

(*The stalemate continues.*)

ALMEDA. *A better shooting guard than me?*

INEZ. *Al!*

C'mon, jump ball!

(*A beat and then* INEZ *steps in to take the ball away.*)

AL!

(ALMEDA *leans into* JEAN.)

ALMEDA. Just try and take shooting guard from me, Jean. You won't live long enough to repent.

(ALMEDA *exits.* JEAN *dusts herself off.*)

JEAN. She ought not speak that way.

> (INEZ *hands* JEAN *the ball.*)

INEZ. I heard you talk a fair bit of trash, too.

JEAN. I just don't know why you bother with that...baby.

INEZ. No bother. You need a routine.
> The number of times you bounce the ball.
> The way you drag your feet.
> Should be the same before every shot.

> (JEAN *scrapes off the bottom of her shoes and dribbles three times.*)

INEZ. Whisper something.
> A secret.

> (JEAN *whispers something, then shoots.*)

> You see?
> Can't think on anything but the game when you're playing.
> That's the point.

JEAN. That works?

INEZ. I think all day long on falling corn prices.
> And the six little ones who got nowhere to go if we lose the farm.
> And then for a whole hour, I forget.

JEAN. Your secret.

INEZ. Small town, that's no secret.

JEAN. I see.

INEZ. Y'know.
> Al's not a baby.
> No need to think of her that way.

JEAN. Oh, yeah?
> What do you think of Almeda as?

INEZ. A friend.

JEAN. Right.

> (JEAN *lines up a shot.*)

> (*A long beat.*)

INEZ. I'm not ape.

>I see the way she looks sometimes.

>At me.

JEAN. Sweet.

>*(INEZ looks at her.)*

INEZ. Yes.

>So?

>I have six underfoot so I don't deserve anything nice?

JEAN. I'm just asking.

INEZ. There's a boy over in Humboldt who I let look sweet at me, too.

>Charles.

>He's got the longest eyelashes you ever saw on a boy.

JEAN. You're getting close enough for eyelashes.

>*(INEZ laughs it off.)*

INEZ. It's six hours to Humboldt.

>I can only make the trip once every three months.

>What about you?

JEAN. What *about* me?

INEZ. Eyelashes.

JEAN. I'm here to help my Uncle Malcolm.

INEZ. The dresses are nice, but worn.

>You talk soft, but your hands are just as hard as mine.

>There's more to this story.

>*(A beat. JEAN decides to confide.)*

JEAN. A few of the dresses came direct from the store.

>The rest were worn by other girls before me.

INEZ. You lifted 'em?

JEAN. No.

>After my father died, we had to take in laundry. Sometimes people forget or can't pay to pick up the wash.

INEZ. And then – ?

JEAN. One day, my mother found a meal ticket.

The marrying kind.

INEZ. The type of meal ticket only valid for one.

JEAN. I got a train ticket instead.

His treat.

I think there was also something wired to my Uncle Malcolm for my keep.

INEZ. And that's it, then?

You're here to stay.

JEAN. My grave town.

No notion of where my mother's moved off to.

I'll die here and word of it will never leave the town limits.

(JEAN *passes the ball to* INEZ *who does her ritual: Two very quick, low dribbles, a whisper, and then a shot.*)

LURLENE. *(offstage)* Jean!

INEZ. Still room for optimism.

Hazel Shoots used to say:

When you make more baskets than you miss, life feels worth living.

(LURLENE *and* PUPPY *enter in uniform bloomers and middies, clothing in hand.*)

LURLENE. Jean, we got a uniform for you.

INEZ. I oughta return to chores.

(INEZ *exits.*)

JEAN. A uniform?

Really?

LURLENE. Yes, *really.*

Game's in Crooked Pick next week.

(LURLENE *helps* JEAN *into heavy, over-the-knee bloomers and a huge white middy with a floppy collar and a crest over* JEAN's *head.*)

(to JEAN:*)* Here we go.

PUPPY. We found it in the bottom of the class cupboard.

> I've been keeping mine there since Mother said shorts were unladylike.
>
> She has no idea.
>
> It's very wicked.

LURLENE. Puppy, darling, you got no notion what the word *wicked* means.

PUPPY. Speaking of:

> I scrub the dust out from under my fingernails.
>
> But a little always stays.

LURLENE. What of it, Pup?

PUPPY. Mother will put her foot down if I can't keep bleached and clean.

LURLENE. *(Looking* JEAN *up and down:)* Lord, that middy has to be as old as my ma.

PUPPY. It *is* a little larger.

LURLENE. You could cut four of ours out of it.

> But it'll have to do.
>
> Mr. Dibbit won't buy us any more like he used to.

PUPPY. That's nothing to do with me.

LURLENE. A little less fabric would be more fetching.

> Better show off the figure.

JEAN. Thank you for your trouble.

LURLENE. Those your only shoes?

> *(*JEAN *nods.)*

> Then you'll have to play in stocking feet.

PUPPY. You won't have time to buy All-Stars.

LURLENE. Or cash.

> Keep it slow or you'll slip.

JEAN. Can't say I feel ready for a game.

PUPPY. Your luck it's only *Crooked Pick.*

LURLENE. They make Inez look talented.

> *(to* JEAN*:)* And they'll make *you* look experienced.

PUPPY. We're not losing to *Crooked Pick.*

> *(Lights shift.)*

Seven

(The sound of a small crowd and an official's whistle.)

HAUNT JOHNNY. You're losing to *Crooked Pick?*
Crooked Pick!?

(A lower transition-like light up as:)

(ALMEDA *dribbles downcourt like a bull on a fastbreak.*
JEAN *breaks in front of her; throughout the following, she*
slips in her stocking feet. **LURLENE, INEZ,** *and* **PUPPY**
run behind.)

(ALMEDA *slows down just inside the perimeter. She sees*
JEAN *inside the key.)*

HAUNT JOHNNY. Clock's running down!

JEAN. I've got the shot.

(ALMEDA *stops dribbling. It looks as if she might pass*
to **JEAN.** *)*

HAUNT JOHNNY. *Look at Jean!*

JEAN. Almeda, I'm open!

(Instead of passing, **ALMEDA** *takes a long shot and*
misses. [This should be reminiscent of the transition
moments in which **ALMEDA** *has refused to pass to*
JEAN. *])*

HAUNT JOHNNY. *Goddamnit, Al!*

(JEAN *gets the rebound and passes out to* **PUPPY.** *)*

Run the play!

(PUPPY *dribbles and passes to* **LURLENE,** *who shoots*
flashily and misses.)

Make the shot!

(The buzzer sounds. Bright lights up.)

What was that?

Why are you losing to Crooked Pick!

(The girls walk back to **HAUNT JOHNNY.** *)*

HAUNT JOHNNY. Lurlene, this is a *basketball game,* not a modeling contest. Stop shooting like you're posing!

LURLENE. You trying to tell me I looked good?

HAUNT JOHNNY. Inez, you gotta move faster.

You look like you got lead strapped to your ankles. Jean, buy a pair of goddamn All-Stars.

JEAN. Yes, sir.

HAUNT JOHNNY. You're gonna slide into the heating stove. And Puppy!

(**PUPPY** *looks up.*)

PUPPY. Yes?

HAUNT JOHNNY. You look like you're trying to hide out there.

PUPPY. I am.

HAUNT JOHNNY. You're in *Crooked Pick!*

Almeda.

ALMEDA. Coach.

HAUNT JOHNNY. There's no accident to Babe Dublin playing the shooting guard.

ALMEDA. No, Coach.

HAUNT JOHNNY. Why's that?

ALMEDA. Because she's the big scorer.

HAUNT JOHNNY. Babe Dublin plays shooting guard because she keeps her head.

Keep your head, Al –

Or you won't keep the position come next week.

(**HAUNT JOHNNY** *turns to go.*)

Clean up and get in the car.

We got a long road ahead.

(**HAUNT JOHNNY** *exits.*)

(**INEZ, PUPPY, JEAN,** *and* **ALMEDA** *pull clothing over their uniforms.*)

ALMEDA. Babe Dublin averages 16 points a game for the Ballers.

She ain't no selfless martyr.

Why should I be?

JEAN. You might pass, Almeda.

ALMEDA. I'm the best shooter.

JEAN. You *hog* the ball.

ALMEDA. You know *nothing* about basketball.

LURLENE. Doesn't make her wrong, Al.

JEAN. You see?

PUPPY. You don't have to take every shot.

(**ALMEDA** *bounces the oxblood basketball.*)

ALMEDA. Stiff off.
I'm the only one who deserves this basketball.

(**ALMEDA** *exits with the basketball, seething.*)

INEZ. She just wants to win.
So she works herself over.

JEAN. On court and off.

(**LURLENE** *scans the hall.*)

LURLENE. Not much in the way of male prospects.
Makes Poor Prairie look like fertile ground.

(**JEAN** *looks at her leather shoes, as she pulls them on.*)

JEAN. How much do All-Stars cost?

INEZ. Two dollars and thirty cents.

JEAN. Are they worth that kind of dough?

INEZ. Ask Pup.
She's the only one who has a pair without holes.
She's also the fastest.

PUPPY. The more expensive your sneakers, the better you play.
It's fact.

LURLENE. Oh, hold on.
There's a promising lead.

JEAN. So money can buy you a better game?

(**LURLENE** *ties up her uniform top under her breasts, exposing her midriff, and rolls up the hem of her shorts to make them as short as possible.*)

LURLENE. Hello there.

PUPPY. *(looks out)* Lurlene, he looks to be 10 years old.

LURLENE. Maybe I'm making an investment in the future.

JEAN. But how do you get money?

INEZ. The barnstorming teams sell tickets.

PUPPY. They wear the most unladylike uniforms.

INEZ. Babe's no stupe.

She starts the Ballers to get her own money.

JEAN. I want my own shorts.

INEZ. And all new All-Stars.

JEAN. Direct from the store.

LURLENE. So, why don't we do it, too?

INEZ. What?

LURLENE. Charge admission.

And play…in scanty uniforms!

INEZ. Lurlene, who would pay admission to a high school game?

LURLENE. Men.

INEZ. In Poor Prairie?

JEAN. Men wouldn't travel for just high school girls' basketball.

LURLENE. But they might travel for high school girls playing basketball in nearly no clothes.

PUPPY. I don't want to disappoint, but –

INEZ. That's the apest idea I ever heard.

(**ALMEDA** *stalks on, pulling* **HAUNT JOHNNY** *behind.*)

ALMEDA. Coach has something to say.

(**JEAN, LURLENE, INEZ,** *and* **PUPPY** *turn.* **ALMEDA** *looks at* **HAUNT JOHNNY.**)

Go ahead.

HAUNT JOHNNY. Al and I were out in the car talking.

ALMEDA. He called me selfish.

HAUNT JOHNNY. I simply said:

A shooting guard has an eye on the whole game.

ALMEDA. *(mocking)* Keep your head.

HAUNT JOHNNY. The way Jean does.

LURLENE. Jean?

PUPPY. She's only been playing a week.

ALMEDA. Nobody wants Jean.

HAUNT JOHNNY. Is that true?

ALMEDA. Tell him, Inez.

HAUNT JOHNNY. You think you're playing as a team?

ALMEDA. Inez?!?

INEZ. Maybe sometimes you could give somebody else a chance.

(**ALMEDA** *turns away from her.*)

ALMEDA. Jean thinks she could do better?

HAUNT JOHNNY. So.
Let her play you for it.

ALMEDA. That ain't even a challenge.

HAUNT JOHNNY. Jean?
You want to win?

JEAN. Worse than I ever counted on.

ALMEDA. Then let's play.

JEAN. 1-on-1.

ALMEDA. 1-on-4.
They ain't stood up *for* me?
Let 'em play against me.

(**HAUNT JOHNNY** *waves* **PUPPY, INEZ,** *and* **LURLENE** *into place.*)

HAUNT JOHNNY. We'll play to 6.
(to **JEAN***:)* An eye on the whole game.

(**HAUNT JOHNNY** *gives* **ALMEDA** *first possession.* **JEAN** *guards her man-to-man,* **PUPPY** *hangs back a little.* **LURLENE** *and* **INEZ** *defend the basket.* **ALMEDA** *dribbles a few times and puts it up;* **JEAN** *is able to block at least one shot. In contrast, when* **JEAN** *and the other players get possession, they pass and run plays that end with* **JEAN** *scoring.* (**LURLENE, PUPPY,** *and* **INEZ** *praise her,* *astonished, when she does: "Nice shot, **JEAN**" etc.) **JEAN** should win.)*

HAUNT JOHNNY. That's 6 to *(insert number **ALMEDA** makes here).*

There's your answer, Almeda.

Jean plays shooting guard.

*(**ALMEDA** storms out. **JEAN** looks at the ball as **LURLENE**, **PUPPY**, and **INEZ** look at her, surprised.)*

LURLENE. Jean!

INEZ. Quicker than we counted on.

*(**INEZ** exits after **ALMEDA**.)*

JEAN. *(deflecting)* You all played a good game.

HAUNT JOHNNY. Let's get on the road.

LURLENE. Shotgun!

*(**PUPPY**, **LURLENE**, and **INEZ** exit. **HAUNT JOHNNY** looks at **JEAN**.)*

JEAN. I'll be there directly.

HAUNT JOHNNY. Good girl.

(He exits.)

*(**JEAN** looks back down at the basketball.)*

(She dribbles, tentatively.)

JEAN. Twenty-six beats for a half minute…

(She stops dribbling, overcome.)

More than my heart will hold out.

But what if my heart could hold out?

What if.

Poor Prairie.

Didn't have to be my grave town?

(She dribbles, tentatively, again.)

(Blackout.)

End of Act One

Eight

(A light up on **JEAN**, *now dribbling expertly. She wears a new, more revealing uniform and a pair of brand new All-Stars. She is a bit plumper than before.)*

JEAN. *(referring to her aggressive dribbling)* Twenty-six beats for a half-minute!

(The sound of **JEAN**'s *dribbling is suddenly compounded by the offstage rumble of feet and hands.)*

We've been playing 15 ½ weeks.

I can do better.

I can do:

Fifty-two beats.

*(***JEAN*** dribbles faster as* **LURLENE**, **INEZ**, **PUPPY**, *and* **ALMEDA** *enter; they all wear matching scanty uniforms and Converse.)*

Four Corner Chest.

(Everyone gets into formation for the drill.)

(Throw in as useful:)

C'mon, hands ready.

Your hearts will hold out!

You're open!

Come on, get open!

(If a ball gets away from them:)

Hustle!

We need to keep the count!

Diamond Dribble.

(Drill begins.)

(Throw in as useful:) Eyes up, ball low!

Keep the count!

Come on, protect the ball.

And Lay-ups!

(*Drill begins.*)

(*Throw in as useful:*)

Put it up.

Let's hustle.

Come on, lay it up!

Use the backboard!

Nice shot!

(*As* **JEAN** *is going in for a lay-up,* **ALMEDA** *knocks* **JEAN**'*s shot out of the hoop with Hazel's ball.*)

Almeda!

You'll repent that with suicides later.

C'mon, let's keep the count:

Five-Man Weave!

(*The sound of an official's whistle; the lights shift and* **JEAN** *passes the ball to* **ALMEDA** *without looking at her.* **ALMEDA** *shoots the ball. If the shot goes in, the buzzer sounds immediately. If she misses, the buzzer sounds when a rebound shot is sunk. The girls celebrate at the buzzer.*)

(**HAUNT JOHNNY** *appears on the sidelines, clapping.*)

PUPPY. Good game!

INEZ. First time we've beat Watertown since Hazel played.

LURLENE. And I'll wager she didn't look this good doing it.

(**LURLENE** *demonstrates the new uniform's range of movement.*)

HAUNT JOHNNY. You all played well.

ALMEDA. Woulda played better with our old uniforms.

JEAN. We've won eight of the last nine.

I'd say the new uniforms are serving us well.

(**JEAN** *pulls at her tight uniform top.*)

HAUNT JOHNNY. Key is to focus on the next two games.

JEAN. Two more wins.

HAUNT JOHNNY. And we'll play Humboldt in the County Championship.

JEAN. Win County?

LURLENE. And we'll go Downstate!

HAUNT JOHNNY. But we'll have to keep our heads to get there.

Everyone ought to bundle up and go home to bed.

I don't want to hear about anybody taking the run of the plains tonight, you understand?

PUPPY. Yes, Coach!

(*HAUNT JOHNNY exits.*)

ALMEDA. *(mocking) Go home to bed.*
You understand?

JEAN. Almeda, you will mind those instructions.

ALMEDA. *Urgh!*

I'm so tired of you.

And this uniform.

JEAN. Lurlene designed them.

LURLENE. You're welcome, darling.

ALMEDA. A real player wouldn't strut around like this.

And you.

Tarting yourself out in the tightest one.

INEZ. Al, that's enough.

LURLENE. I let out her seams.

She has a magical growing bust.

INEZ. That's the winter.

Lighter work.

Less lifting.

JEAN. Almeda, come along.

LURLENE. I wish I'd experience some further development.

I do the exercises from *The Red Book*, but nothing –

ALMEDA. I'm walkin' by myself.

JEAN. You are home in 10 minutes.

(ALMEDA exits.)

Or else.

(JEAN exits. The sound of a basketball dribbling in the distance. LURLENE squints out at the sound.)

LURLENE. Sounds like someone isn't heeding his own instructions.

(INEZ helps PUPPY bundle up.)

Pup, you think you can sneak home by yourself tonight?

PUPPY. But, Lurlene, my bedroom window –

Even when I stand on my very tippy toes, I can't reach –

INEZ. I can give her a boost inside.

LURLENE. As a reward, I'll have a new story for you both tomorrow.

PUPPY. Will it be scandalous?

LURLENE. Aren't they always, darling?

(LURLENE exits in the direction HAUNT JOHNNY left.)

INEZ. Almost ready, Puppy?

PUPPY. That was a good game!

INEZ. Mhhhm.

PUPPY. This *is* a good game. And the uniforms!

I don't even mind that they're not ladylike –

Because they tell the world: We are a TEAM.

I used to envy you your brothers and sisters, Inez.

Lucky Inez to always have somebody to play with.

INEZ. Puppy, I need to ask you.

A letter arrived from your father yesterday.

PUPPY. What?

INEZ. A collection letter.

PUPPY. Oh.

INEZ. Puppy, dear, you have to tell him we're paying as much as we can.

PUPPY. That's nothing to do with me.

INEZ. We have *nowhere* to go if we lose the farm.

PUPPY. I imagine you should just give the bank the money
you said you would.

INEZ. It's not just the principal owed the bank anymore.
There are fees in addition now.

PUPPY. Maybe there's a little money tucked away
somewhere?

INEZ. You can't be serious.

PUPPY. Well, my mother always keeps a little in a jar for
small expenses.

Maybe.

(A beat.)

INEZ. Maybe.

(A shift:)

C'mon now, let's get you home.

(INEZ starts to lead her off.)

PUPPY. I'm barely even sleepy.

(PUPPY and INEZ exit.)

*(Sounds of the bouncing basketball grow closer and
HAUNT JOHNNY comes into view, dribbling. LURLENE
approaches from the opposite direction.)*

LURLENE.Well, what are the odds, Mr. Oddment?
You taking the run of the plains tonight?

HAUNT JOHNNY. Headed home to bed, Lurlene.
You ought to be, too.

LURLENE. Is that an invitation?

HAUNT JOHNNY. You know it isn't.

LURLENE. You want some company for the walk?

HAUNT JOHNNY. Good night, Lurlene.

LURLENE. I'm a better looker than half the ladies in *The
Red Book.*
You can't look at me and say you don't see that.

(HAUNT JOHNNY stops to look at her.)

HAUNT JOHNNY. I look at you, Lurlene, and I see Terrence
Lonestead.

Sixteen years old and standing tall.

On top of the world at the bottom of the lane –
Throwing up the most spectacular hook shot.

LURLENE. I don't understand.

HAUNT JOHNNY. I see that you just might be more than
your nail paint, Lurlene.

(*A beat.*)

LURLENE. Did Terrence ever make it Downstate?

HAUNT JOHNNY. We were knocked out the round before.
Sophomore year.

LURLENE. So, if we win the next two games –

HAUNT JOHNNY. We're in the County Championships –

LURLENE. And if we beat Humboldt at County –

HAUNT JOHNNY. We make it Downstate –

LURLENE. And I'll have overdone him.

HAUNT JOHNNY. That's so, I s'pose.

LURLENE. Lord, if I just make it past my seventeenth
birthday, I'll have overdone him.

HAUNT JOHNNY. I s'pose that's also so.

LURLENE. I gotta get Downstate.

HAUNT JOHNNY. Then how about this for a trade?
I'll do my level to get you there.

LURLENE. In return?

HAUNT JOHNNY. You want it for more than just a tiara.

(**HAUNT JOHNNY** *passes her the ball. He exits as she
starts dribbling, athletically and aggressively.*)

(*The sound of a crowd begins to filter in from a distance.*)

(**LURLENE** *stops to look at her fingernails and notices
that her polish has chipped. A beat. She decides not to
care.*)

LURLENE. Ah, stiff it.

(**LURLENE** *dribbles again.*)

(*Lights shift.*)

Nine

(As the lights come up, the sounds of a rumbling crowd grow closer and are joined by the squeaking of sneakers on a waxed wooden floor and an official's whistle.)

*(**PUPPY** stands alone, bouncing nervously as a warm-up. Every time the crowd noise surges, her eyes bulge out of her head.)*

PUPPY. I don't want to disappoint.

Oh my, I don't want to disappoint, but.

Mother says no more basketball.

*(**ALMEDA** enters, running.)*

Al! I need to tell you –

ALMEDA. Not now.

*(**PUPPY** grabs her arm.)*

PUPPY. I know it's the County Championships, but Al –
ALMEDA. I can't.

My *uniform.*

I can't play.

*(**ALMEDA** breaks free of **PUPPY**'s grip and exits, running.)*

PUPPY. That isn't fair.

I can't play.

*(**LURLENE** enters.)*

LURLENE. *(offstage)* Puppy!
PUPPY. I should never have come to Humboldt.
LURLENE. Puppy!

You are missing the *BOYS'* game!

Third quarter.

And then we'll be up next!

PUPPY. Lurlene, I didn't want to get in the car.
LURLENE. Oh my god, Puppy!

The floor in there shines like gold.

Waxed wood.

PUPPY. And I didn't expect:

That there would be *so many* people watching.

LURLENE. Y'know, there are all these girls in the stands, clapping and wearing nail paint.

PUPPY. A *CROWD*.

LURLENE. Once upon a time, Pup, I just wanted to be one of 'em.

But I see:

I belong *on* the court.

(**INEZ** *enters.*)

PUPPY. The thing is, Lurlene, Mother told me –

LURLENE. Hold it, Pup.

Inez, you're missing a great game!

INEZ. What?

LURLENE. I didn't see you in there watching the first half of the boys' game.

INEZ. I went for a walk.

LURLENE. But isn't Charles playing?

INEZ. I've seen him from the bleachers enough.

LURLENE. Oh, no, Inez.

Did Charles bust it up with you?

INEZ. No, just.

Before the game.

I saw him.

Up close.

LURLENE. Okay…?

INEZ. In my memory?

His eyelashes were longer, I think.

And his breath was.

Sweeter.

And so was the way he looked at me.

LURLENE. Cheer up, Inez!

We just gotta get Downstate.

How many times you tell me yourself:

You can't think about any of that when you're playing.

(A buzzer is heard offstage.)

PUPPY. Oh, no. That's – ?

LURLENE. Fourth quarter.

INEZ. We ought to stretch.

LURLENE. Let's head inside.

    *(**INEZ** and **LURLENE** start to exit.)*

PUPPY. But Lurlene –

LURLENE. C'mon, Pup.

PUPPY. I can't!

    *(**PUPPY** sighs, runs after them.)*

    Lurlene!

    I *can't* play!

    (The crowd noises grow momentarily closer.)

JEAN. *(offstage)* Almeda!

    *(**JEAN** enters, running.)*

    Almeda?

    *(**JEAN** circles the stage, listening. A noise offstage.)*

    Almeda!

    *(**JEAN** runs to the noise.)*

    Almeda!

    I know you're in there.

    (more noise)

    You ought not to have run away from me.

    You hear me?

ALMEDA. *(offstage)* I ain't comin' out!

JEAN. Don't be a baby.

    (A beat.)

ALMEDA. *(offstage)* I looked for Inez.

JEAN. You got me.

    *(**ALMEDA** emerges from offstage, wearing overalls over her uniform.)*

ALMEDA. I don't need no mother.

JEAN. What is it?

ALMEDA. My uniform.

JEAN. What?

> (ALMEDA *hugs the overall bib to her chest as* JEAN *crosses to her.*)

ALMEDA. My…*uniform.*

JEAN. Let me take a look.

> (JEAN *grabs* ALMEDA *firmly.* ALMEDA *pulls the bib away from her chest and* JEAN *looks down her overalls.*)
>
> Oh.
>
> *That.*
>
> (ALMEDA *grabs the bib and stomps away, back to* JEAN. JEAN *winces.*)

ALMEDA. It's all over my shorts and it ain't even stopped yet.

Why won't it STOP?

> (*A beat.*)

Jean?

JEAN. Oh.

ALMEDA. I'm dying.

JEAN. You're not dying.

ALMEDA. Tug off.

JEAN. It's a sign, actually.

Of life.

ALMEDA. But it's all over my shorts.

How do I get it off my shorts?

> (*A beat.*)

JEAN?

JEAN. We can, uh. Spot clean them.

> (JEAN *starts to lead* ALMEDA *offstage, but she doesn't budge.*)

ALMEDA. Everyone will know.

JEAN. No, uh –

> I'll rig you up a belt.

ALMEDA. Certain?

JEAN. The stains I've taken out in my time?

> This is nothing.
>
> Go on, take them off, and start soaking.
>
> I'll be right in.

> (**ALMEDA** *exits.* **JEAN** *winces.* **JEAN** *puts a hand on her stomach.*)

> I was just a bit…*unwell.*
>
> How could I not trust my count?

HAUNT JOHNNY. *(offstage)* Jean?

> (**JEAN** *pulls her hand away from her stomach, quickly as* **HAUNT JOHNNY** *enters, pamphlet in hand.*)

JEAN. I'm headed in shortly.

HAUNT JOHNNY. Jean.

> Keep your head in there.
>
> Could be our last best option.

> (**HAUNT JOHNNY** *hands her the pamphlet.*)

> A lady in white gloves handed it to me outside the square.

> (**JEAN** *looks at the pamphlet.*)

JEAN. I see.

HAUNT JOHNNY. The Committee on Play's convening in the Capitol.

JEAN. Leading society ladies.

HAUNT JOHNNY. Timing's unlucky, but if we play –

JEAN. Overexertion and impediments to childbearing.

HAUNT JOHNNY. I need you to go out there and play, Jean.

> (**JEAN** *nods.*)

JEAN. Like it's the last basketball game of my life.

HAUNT JOHNNY. Good girl.

(**INEZ, LURLENE,** *and* **PUPPY** *re-enter and the sound of the crowd grows closer.*)

(*to* **EVERYONE:**) We'll circle in two.

(**HAUNT JOHNNY** *exits.*)

INEZ. (*to* **JEAN:**) You all set?

JEAN. Just a moment.

INEZ. That's all we have.

(**JEAN** *exits in the direction* **ALMEDA** *left.*)

LURLENE. Any minute now!

PUPPY. Lurlene, I have to tell you.

LURLENE. We'll be *on court.*

This is better than *The Red Book.*

PUPPY. LURLENE!

I don't want to disappoint, but.

I can't play today.

LURLENE. Don't be foolish, Pup.

PUPPY. Mother says no more basketball.

LURLENE. No more basketball?

PUPPY. I heard her whispering on the telephone.

News from the Committee, I think.

About the team.

INEZ. What news?

PUPPY. Something about Coach, I don't know.

But she put down her foot this morning.

I've crossed her already, just coming to Humboldt.

LURLENE. You shoulda said something earlier.

PUPPY. I *TRIED.*

You pulled me into the car.

INEZ. But, Puppy, you're part of the team.

(**ALMEDA** *and* **JEAN** *re-enter as the sound of a buzzer comes closer.*)

INEZ. That's us.

(**HAUNT JOHNNY** *enters.*)

HAUNT JOHNNY. Circle up.

> (**INEZ, LURLENE, ALMEDA,** *and* **JEAN** *put their hands in a circle.*)

LURLENE. C'mon, Pup.

PUPPY. I *told* you:

No more basketball.

Or else.

ALMEDA. We can't play with four.

INEZ. Puppy, we're a team.

You're one of us.

> (**LURLENE** *walks over to take* **PUPPY** *by the arm.*)

LURLENE. She's fibbing – she'll play.

> (**INEZ** *crosses to them.*)

PUPPY. NO.

I *won't.*

> (**ALMEDA** *makes it part way to them. The three of them pull at* **PUPPY**.)

ALMEDA. Puppy, it's time.

LURLENE. It's us or her.

> (**PUPPY** *struggles a little against* **LURLENE***'s grip.* **INEZ** *and* **ALMEDA** *help her.* **HAUNT JOHNNY** *looks at* **JEAN**.)

HAUNT JOHNNY. *(still looking at* **JEAN***)* That's enough.

ALMEDA. If we don't go RIGHT now –

JEAN. We'll forfeit.

> (*The buzzer sounds again and the girls pull* **PUPPY** *into the circle; she looks out at the crowd, terrified and exposed.*)

HAUNT JOHNNY. On three: Downstate.

> (*The girls scream and throw their arms back.*)

JEAN. Play like it's the last basketball game of your life.

> (*The sound of the crowd grows deafeningly loud and suddenly close as the girls enter the gymnasium.*)

(Lights shift into transition, then game mode. It's the last moment of the game. The clock is stopped and JEAN *is at the free throw line. The rest of the team is lined up on either side of the lane.)*

(Unseen bleachers shake with the crowd's stomps and the low rumble of focus-breaking cries.)

HAUNT JOHNNY. Two seconds on the clock.

JEAN. One point worth one...

(JEAN *does her free throw routine. Time is suspended as the sound of the crowd shifts slightly toward the poetic. She shoots. If she makes it, the clock restarts and* **HAUNT JOHNNY** *counts it down ("And two, one – ") before the buzzer sounds and the crowd erupts and the girls celebrate and the lights shift. If she misses, she shoots again – and makes it this time! – before the clock restarts, etc.)*

HAUNT JOHNNY. 31-30!

(As the lights shift, the sounds of immediate post-game celebration evolve into the sounds of a night-long party.)

Ten

(As **JEAN** *enters, the sound of squealing girls grows farther away. She still wears her warm-up suit and All-Stars with a jacket thrown over her.)*

(She has a hand on her belly.)

JEAN. Eleven million two hundred and thirty-two thousand beats for these five months.

*(***HAUNT JOHNNY*** approaches in hat and coat.)*

HAUNT JOHNNY. I was wondering where you'd gotten off to.

*(***JEAN*** looks down.)*

They've broken out another jug of that corn whiskey inside.

You woulda thought they'd drunk enough to kill on the ride home from Humboldt this morning –

But it takes a lot to knock out your cousin.

JEAN. I'm not good company right now.

HAUNT JOHNNY. I'm never good company.

*(***HAUNT JOHNNY*** hands her his hat.)*

It's cold.

JEAN. This is the end.

HAUNT JOHNNY. We're going Downstate.

Another month of play.

We got a whole tournament ahead.

*(***JEAN*** shakes her head.)*

JEAN. This is my grave town.

(The light begins to change in anticipation of the sunset.)

HAUNT JOHNNY. You can make it in this, Jean.

You hear me?

You're starting late, but you can make it.

Industrial leagues or better yet professional.

You're nice and tall with good, evenly-strong hands
and hard legs and the head to play any man alive.

And you learn – you can give yourself over to coaching,
Jean.

You are the one in 5,000 –

That's – ?

JEAN. .02%.

HAUNT JOHNNY. You are the .02% of grown people who
get to *play*.

For a living.

You can keep playing, Jean.

(A beat.)

Babe'll be playing Antler Stadium around tournament
time.

We could get her on the train up to the Capitol and
get you seen…

You want to meet Babe Dublin?

JEAN. So much worse than I ever counted on.

But.

If you knew me.

Truly.

You wouldn't.

HAUNT JOHNNY. I know you, Jean.

(A beat.)

JEAN. I was sent away because my mother found a meal
ticket.

HAUNT JOHNNY. The marrying kind.

JEAN. Not at first, he wasn't.

At first.

He was sweeter on me than he was on her.

HAUNT JOHNNY. I see.

JEAN. So, I was sent away.

HAUNT JOHNNY. That's not so –

JEAN. That's not all.

HAUNT JOHNNY. So?

I did my learning in prison.

Not teacher's college.

JEAN. The South.

(**HAUNT JOHNNY** *nods.*)

You break out?

HAUNT JOHNNY. No.

Early release due to overcrowding.

JEAN. You mean to do what you did?

HAUNT JOHNNY. No.

(*The dust around them glows gold in the setting sunlight and* **JEAN** *inhales.*)

JEAN. Like whiskey flavor pipe smoke and cloves and orange peel and snow.

HAUNT JOHNNY. The way the sun smells.

JEAN. And I'm tied in.

(**JEAN** *turns to him, reaches out to touch his face.*)

Before I can say "help".

(**JEAN** *kisses him. They stand close for a long beat.* **JEAN** *exhales.*)

The more to this story is.

(*A beat.*)

If my count's not wrong –

HAUNT JOHNNY. When's your count been wrong?

JEAN. Never. By my count.

It's been 22 ½ weeks since. 18 til.

I'll give birth.

Another month and it's certain I'll show.

By my 16th birthday, everyone will know.

The week of the tournament.

HAUNT JOHNNY. Oh.

JEAN. Like I said:

Sweeter on me than on her.

HAUNT JOHNNY. I see.

JEAN. So, go ahead:
>Tell me I can keep playing.
>Tell me you'll stick with me.

ALMEDA. Coach!
>Come inside quick!

>(**ALMEDA** *bursts in.*)

JEAN. Almeda.

>(**JEAN** *springs up and exits inside;* **HAUNT JOHNNY** *doesn't move.*)

ALMEDA. *Jean?*

HAUNT JOHNNY. *(eyes still on* **JEAN***)* Go back inside, Al.

ALMEDA. I see.

HAUNT JOHNNY. I don't think you do.

ALMEDA. Her skills at shooting guard.

HAUNT JOHNNY. Al –

ALMEDA. And you called *me* selfish?

HAUNT JOHNNY. Go back inside.

ALMEDA. Then you better come with –
>It's Mrs. Dibbit.

HAUNT JOHNNY. What?

ALMEDA. She's here.

>(*A shrieking whistle that might be a girl's scream. Lights shift.*)

Eleven

(Lights up on **LURLENE** *and* **JEAN** *in the classroom. Neither looks like they've slept.)*

LURLENE. I heard screams a half-mile away.

JEAN. It's the flatness.

LURLENE. They killed her.
They killed Puppy.

JEAN. Don't say that.

*(***ALMEDA*** enters.)*

LURLENE. Puppy?
Oh…*Al.*
I'll be outside smoking.
I'm so worried, I may even *light* my cigarette.

*(***LURLENE*** exits.)*

JEAN. Almeda, I have to tell you –

*(***ALMEDA*** turns.)*

ALMEDA. Only took you four-and-a-half months.
I dreamed my *whole life.*
On Downstate.
On meeting Babe Dublin.
On a brand new basketball.
And it only took you four-and-a-half months to take it all away.
Now I know how.

JEAN. Almeda, I'm –

INEZ. *(offstage)* Jean!

*(***INEZ*** enters.)*

Still no word?

ALMEDA. *He* ain't shown his face neither.

INEZ. Poor Pup.

(A car engine offstage. **LURLENE** *runs on.)*

LURLENE. She's here.

ALMEDA. Puppy!

LURLENE. She's alive.

(PUPPY enters, clean and neatly dressed. She carries a newspaper clipping in her hand.)

INEZ. Puppy!

(The girls crowd around her. LURLENE tries to give her a hug. PUPPY does not respond.)

ALMEDA. We were worrying on you, Pup!

INEZ. You're not hurt, are you dear?

LURLENE. I heard shrieking.

PUPPY. I'm fine.

(PUPPY shrugs off one of the hands placed on her shoulder.)

LURLENE. You don't seem fine.

ALMEDA. What's wrong with you?

LURLENE. Puppy, what is that?

(PUPPY holds up the newspaper clipping.)

PUPPY. The committee made its recommendations.

(A beat.)

ALMEDA. What'd they say?

INEZ. *(low)* Al, we know what they said.

ALMEDA. I need to hear for myself.
WHAT DID THEY SAY?

(A beat. PUPPY begins reading.)

PUPPY. Representatives to the state assembly of the Committee on Play, Girls Division, cheered on by Mrs. Hoover herself, passed a resolution Monday that will prohibit extramural competition, oppose gate receipts, and ban all travel and publicity for girls' and women's sporting events. Citing physicians' studies and the testimony of leading society ladies, the State Secondary School Principals Association issued a statement of support for the resolution and has begun to pressure area high schools to disband their girls' basketball teams effective immediately.

(A beat.)

INEZ. So that's it, then.

ALMEDA. Why would that be it?

It's a *recommendation*, it's not a law.

We can fight.

INEZ. Al.

ALMEDA. No, why not?

I make more baskets than I miss.

INEZ. Optimism's easier on the court.

ALMEDA. We want this bad enough?

We fight for it.

(JEAN steps closer to ALMEDA.)

(LURLENE, JEAN, ALMEDA, and INEZ face PUPPY.)

PUPPY. I don't want to disappoint, but.

I don't want to fight.

LURLENE. You don't mean that, Pup.

(HAUNT JOHNNY enters.)

PUPPY. Yes, I do.

And if you ever *listened* to me – even just once – you would know that.

I don't think we ought to play basketball.

It's not doing us any good.

I mean, Al:

Who would marry you? You're very nearly not a girl.

And, Inez:

Why bother? You don't have any natural gifts. And anyway, shouldn't you be working to keep your family's farm? Your brothers and sisters are going to end up in a state home, because you were off *playing*, Inez.

And, Lurlene:

You're cheap and vulgar – you think it's winning, but it's not. And your looks are average, everyone but you sees that.

The whole town is laughing at you and your copy of *The Red Book*.

HAUNT JOHNNY. I think you ought to stop talking.

PUPPY. You think you're so clever.

HAUNT JOHNNY. Puppy, *I'm warning*.

PUPPY. So much cleverer than all of Poor Prairie!

That's what you think.

That you can march plain into town –

And nobody'll ask where you've been all these years since you last vagabonded away.

And even if someone did ask, who would answer?

Given that we're all such nobodies as to not know a soul outside Poor Prairie.

Well, figure this, Mr. Oddment, Mother isn't a nobody. Word of you and your sins spread through the Committee.

JEAN. Puppy Dibbit, you clam your mouth.

PUPPY. He's a criminal, you know!

JEAN. He didn't break out.

PUPPY. What does that matter when he got sent up for manslaughter?!

ALMEDA. You have blood on your hands?

JEAN. No.

PUPPY. Yes.

HAUNT JOHNNY. I don't know.

He was still breathing when I walked away.

But. I was taller, a great deal taller, so.

I don't know.

JEAN. He come after you?

HAUNT JOHNNY. And a girl.

No older than you.

(JEAN *is taken aback.*)

JEAN. What were you after with a girl no older than me?

HAUNT JOHNNY. It wasn't that sort of –

PUPPY. He is known to develop *inappropriate* attachments, I'm told.

HAUNT JOHNNY. We were in a grave town down South.
>The Ballers took a game with the kinda team.
>The kinda team that takes games against ladies for the chance to rough one or two up in the rebound.
>Not something I would get any joy to watch.
>So, I went over to the high school to see a girl I'd heard was worth having a look.

LURLENE. For her good Cupid's bow?

HAUNT JOHNNY. For her skills as a shooting guard.

JEAN. Fifteen.
>And-a-half.

HAUNT JOHNNY. It wasn't anything.
>She wasn't anything.
>Not near tall enough.
>But her father come spitting for a fight anyway.

ALMEDA. And you gave it to him.

HAUNT JOHNNY. I didn't run from it.
>Didn't burn my bloody shirt.

PUPPY. Babe Dublin herself turned him in.

HAUNT JOHNNY. If I'da known she would –
>I woulda hustled a pick-up out of town.
>But I never dreamed it of her.
>Babe hadn't ever been the type to sell out the team after a loss.

ALMEDA. Babe Dublin wouldn't turn.
>Not unless you were in the wrong.

HAUNT JOHNNY. She might've thought so.

JEAN. You said she would see me.

HAUNT JOHNNY. She *would've* seen you.
>I swear.

JEAN. And then seen you too.
>You deliver up another girl and all is forgiven?

HAUNT JOHNNY. You weren't just another.

PUPPY. They're gonna run you out of town if you don't run yourself first.

JEAN. I told you to clam it already.

PUPPY. I haven't even begun.

Oh, *no*.

The things I could say about *you*.

You come lately to town, but you ought to be sent away already.

(to the others:) She's not just grown plump, you know. Mother says she's gotten herself in trouble.

INEZ. Puppy.

ALMEDA. Jean?

PUPPY. Open your eyes.

(to **JEAN***:)* Go on and tell them.

Tell them Mother has errored.

Tell them you're *not* in trouble.

ALMEDA. *Jean.*

*(**JEAN** looks at her feet.)*

*(**LURLENE** looks at **HAUNT JOHNNY**.)*

LURLENE. Oh god.

*(**JEAN** exits.)*

PUPPY. He's gone and delivered up another girl.

LURLENE. I KNEW it.

*(**HAUNT JOHNNY** exits.)*

INEZ. No, he couldn't be –

LURLENE. It's not that I might be more than my nail paint, is it?

More accurate to say that his tastes don't run along the lines of nail paint.

He won't shake this.

ALMEDA. Lurlene, you have no notion.

LURLENE. I'll make certain word spreads.

About Jean, too.

(ALMEDA leaps toward LURLENE.)

ALMEDA. You wouldn't –

LURLENE. Just watch me.

(INEZ pulls ALMEDA off her as PUPPY watches.)

INEZ. It's not worth it, Al.

ALMEDA. But Jean –

I'm so ANGRY I don't know what to say.

INEZ. I do.

(to PUPPY:) You are a disappointment.

(All exit separately, leaving PUPPY onstage alone for a moment.)

(In the transition, basketball disappears, as does HAUNT JOHNNY. He takes a last look at Poor Prairie, suitcase and burlap bundle in hand.)

(The sound of a train whistle gives way to a shovel on hard-packed dirt.)

Twelve

*(Lights up on **ALMEDA**, spitting mad, digging desperately with the shovel. She flings dirt behind her until she reaches the doll, then pulls up the doll's dress and pulls out the jar and empties it into her palm – a single coin falls out. **ALMEDA** holds it up, distraught.)*

ALMEDA. Inez!

(No response.)

INEZ!

INEZ, come quick.

*(**INEZ** enters, wearing a housecoat. She looks like she's been crying.)*

INEZ. Shhhh.

Sound travels.

ALMEDA. Where the hell is my money?

INEZ!

INEZ. Not now.

I gotta put the babies down.

ALMEDA. Somebody robbed.

INEZ. It was meant to be a borrowing.

ALMEDA. *You* took my money? Why would you take my money, Inez?

*(**INEZ** shakes her head.)*

INEZ. Trying to stop the dam from overflowing.

Not that it made any difference in the end.

ALMEDA. What're you talking on?

INEZ. The farm, Al.

Mr. Dibbit drew up the papers today.

Fifty years this land was in the family.

And I'm the one to lose it.

ALMEDA. Corn prices ain't your foul.

*(**ALMEDA** hugs **INEZ**.)*

INEZ. My ma wants to try to rent, but they're gonna auction off the equipment.

She won't be able to hang on.

ALMEDA. This is why I come for the money.

Don't care what anybody else is doing, we gotta go Downstate.

(**INEZ** *tries to step out of the embrace.* **ALMEDA** *does not let her go.*)

INEZ. Al.

Tournament's disappeared.

ALMEDA. They can't do that.

(**INEZ** *steps away,* **ALMEDA** *continues to hold her hands.*)

INEZ. Already have.

If you would've come to see me earlier, you would have heard.

(*A beat.*)

ALMEDA. Then hang it.

We'll get out picking up hustles.

We can get a two-on-two game going.

Make our way down to Babe Dublin.

INEZ. Al, I have to tell you –

ALMEDA. It doesn't matter if you're weaker, Inez.

I want it bad enough for both of us.

And we can use that as part of the hustle – let them play just you first.

(**INEZ** *pries* **ALMEDA**'s *fingers off her hand.*)

INEZ. Al, I'm going to Humboldt.

Charles will have me.

ALMEDA. Charles will *have you?*

As if Charles with the sour breath is favoring you with a service?

INEZ. Well.

He is.

I'm going to bring the two youngest with.

ALMEDA. And that's it?

You and Hazel Shoots'll live next door with your no-talent former ball players?

Is that all you want for yourself?

To be a *Has-Been?*

INEZ. Al, Hazel's life looks pretty damn nice to me right now.

ALMEDA. She never plays basketball anymore!

You said so yourself.

(INEZ shrugs.)

INEZ. I'll be 18, Al.

This is what grown-ups do.

They stop playing.

(ALMEDA exits; INEZ watches her go.)

Thirteen

(In low light:)

(JEAN enters, keeping a lantern low.)

(She is now visibly, though not heavily, pregnant; she carries Hazel's shriveled-up basketball.)

JEAN. Five shots.
For these five-and-a-half months.
Better than half.
Is optimism.
Better than half.
Is 3 out of 5.
3 out of 5.
Is worth living for.

(JEAN does her free-throw ritual and shoots.)

(If she makes it:)	*(If she misses:)*
1 for 1.	0 for 1.

(If she makes it:)	*(If she makes this but missed the last:)*	*(If she misses)*
2 for 2.	1 for 2.	0 for 2.

(JEAN does her free-throw ritual and shoots.)

(She should miss if she's made the first two.)	*(Makes this, has made one of first two:)*	*(If she misses)*
2 for 3.	2 for 3.	0 for 3. Then 3 out of 6 is half. Half a life. Could still be worth living for.

(JEAN does her free-throw ritual and shoots.)

(She should miss if she's already made two.)

(HAUNT JOHNNY *enters, burlap bundle in hand, after she has taken four shots. The count might be 2 for 4, 1 for 4, or 0 for 4.*)

HAUNT JOHNNY. I saw you.

(*He rolls the oxblood basketball toward her.* JEAN *turns around, startled. A long beat.*)

JEAN. You are like to be a ghost.

HAUNT JOHNNY. I got down to Correctionville. But I had to turn back.

JEAN. I will blink.

(JEAN *blinks.*)

If anybody were to catch sight of you…

HAUNT JOHNNY. I know.

But I had to.

(JEAN *inhales sharply.*)

You are .02%.

JEAN. I summed that up for you.

HAUNT JOHNNY. I only mean.

You weren't just another.

Good hands, good legs, and a great head.

JEAN. You came back for me?

HAUNT JOHNNY. I had to see you.

(JEAN *rushes toward him.* ALMEDA *enters in the shadows. She looks on, unseen.*)

JEAN. I knew *you* weren't just another.

I knew *you* would stick with me.

(HAUNT JOHNNY *takes a step back from her.*)

HAUNT JOHNNY. *Jean.*

JEAN. I did not tell anyone about the smell of the sun.

HAUNT JOHNNY. Jean.

I have to move on to the next.

JEAN. We could move on together.

HAUNT JOHNNY. You know I can't.

(A beat.)

JEAN. You'll be wanting your ball back.

(She passes the oxblood ball to him, forcefully. **HAUNT JOHNNY** *passes the ball back to her.)*

HAUNT JOHNNY. It's yours.

JEAN. You shouldn't have.

HAUNT JOHNNY. Keep practicing the free throws.

JEAN. They're not free.

HAUNT JOHNNY. Goodbye, Jean.

*(***HAUNT JOHNNY*** *exits;* **JEAN** *watches him go.)*

(A beat.)

*(***ALMEDA*** *steps out; she reaches out to* **JEAN.***)*

ALMEDA. Jean?

*(***JEAN*** *turns away from her.* **ALMEDA** *exits.)*

*(***JEAN*** *bounces the ball violently and screams.)*

(A long beat. She picks the ball back up. If the count was 2 for 4:)

Three out of five.

I have to make.

Three out of five.

Or there's nothing.

Worth living for.

(If the count was anything else:)

My next last best option.

1 out of 1.

It's everything or nothing.

Make 1.

Or life won't be worth living.

*(***JEAN*** *does the routine, wincing as she whispers her secret to herself, and shoots.)*

(The lantern blows out before we can see whether or not she made the shot.)

Fourteen

*(**LURLENE** in her tied-up basketball uniform holds the photograph of Hazel Shoots and a smoked-down cigarette butt.)*

LURLENE. This morning, after I got word from the Humboldt boys' team, I painted my nails again for the first time in six weeks. I am my nail paint, ya know. And then I started thinking up some ideas. Like, I could help the crowd spell things out. In my experience posing, I've come to find out I look best when I'm longest, so I would shape the letters with my body, like…
V-

*(**LURLENE** makes a "V", cigarette and photo still in hand.)*

I-

*(**LURLENE** makes an "I".)*

C-

This one's a little tricky.

*(**LURLENE** makes a "C".)*

T-

*(**LURLENE** makes a "T".)*

You get the notion.
And I been thinking I might get so overstimulated by the excitement that I could kick my leg as high as I can, like…

*(**LURLENE** kicks.)*

And what if I made these shorts over into a skirt and I kicked again, overstimulated by the excitement and –

*(**PUPPY** enters. She wears a white dress and white gloves and a hat. She carries a hatbox.)*

PUPPY. Lurlene.
You have to go.

LURLENE. Pup.

How're you gonna keep that bleached and clean?

It's near unthinkable to preserve white.

PUPPY. Blessedly, I won't have to try.

There are girls who take in laundry in the Capitol.

Lurlene, it would be best if Mother didn't see you.

LURLENE. I just wanted to tell you my story.

I thought you'd like listening –

PUPPY. You're going over to Humboldt then?

LURLENE. I'll be leading the cheers.

PUPPY. Good luck.

LURLENE. Maybe I could send you stories every so often?

If you sent me your address, I could maybe be bothered to write down some of my adventures.

They're always scandalous, darling.

(**PUPPY** *nods. It's unconvincing.*)

PUPPY. Maybe.

And how is Almeda?

Without basketball?

(**LURLENE** *shakes her head. She looks out at the horizon.*)

LURLENE. I ain't seen anybody come out of that house.

Not for days.

I don't know.

Maybe I shouldn't have –

PUPPY. Lurlene, you did the right thing.

Spreading the truth.

Don't let anyone shame you for that.

That man was sick.

LURLENE. I don't know.

PUPPY. No, it's so.

He needed to be run out of town.

And now the uncle has proposed to make her honest.

The moment she turns sixteen.

LURLENE. *(horrified)* What?

PUPPY. He's her mother's sister's widower.

LURLENE. Oh god.

PUPPY. It's not ideal, but I suppose it's appropriate.

LURLENE. *Appropriate?*

PUPPY. How else can she live?

(**LURLENE** *looks out to the house on the horizon, pained.*)

LURLENE. That's not living.

That's not worth –

PUPPY. You can't think like that, Lurlene.

You have to disappoint someone.

(**PUPPY** *exits.* **LURLENE** *looks out; her face is broken, regretful, adult.*)

(*Lights shift.*)

(*The sound of a train whistle, far off.*)

Fifteen

(In the darkness, the sound of the train whistle grows and the rush of a train traveling closer and closer yet. The train passes through and travels farther away.)

(From afar, a single basketball dribbled on hard-packed dirt.)

(The lights come up slowly, as if a sunrise. The dust glows golden as a woman in a traveling suit enters in the distance. She walks, awkwardly, in the heels, carrying a rucksack. She is backlit by the gold light.)

(As she walks closer, we can see that this is **ALMEDA** *in* **JEAN***'s traveling suit from the first scene. It is both too loose and too tight in places on* **ALMEDA***.*

(She trips in the heels.)

ALMEDA. Ah, stiff it.

(She looks around to make sure no one else is around and then takes off the shoes. She digs her toes into the dust.)

(She takes a ticket out of her jacket and looks at it, thrumming it nervously against her hand.)

(She counts on her fingers.)

Four hours to Correctionville plus...

(She counts on her fingers.)

Five-and-a-half hours to the Capitol plus...

(She counts on her fingers. As she counts, **JEAN***, wearing* **HAUNT JOHNNY***'s hat and carrying the round burlap bundle enters at a distance.)*

Seven hours to the Antler Stadium.

(She counts on her fingers.)

Sums up to...sixteen-and-a-half hours til Babe's Ballers.

JEAN. *(softly)* I saw you.

(**ALMEDA** *stuffs the ticket back into her jacket and jams her feet back into the heels.*)

Creep out.

Or I thought I did.

Wasn't sure it was you.

ALMEDA. Trying to look the lady.

JEAN. You look nice.

And tall.

ALMEDA. You don't mind?

JEAN. No.

It's a traveling suit.

I'm not going anywhere.

But you needn't have snuck out.

ALMEDA. I didn't want to wake you.

I know sleep's been hard enough to come by.

JEAN. *Al.*

ALMEDA. And here I was grown accustomed to Almeda.

JEAN. There was a little bit of Downstate money leftover.

I put it in view to a purpose.

But it can't have covered more than the ticket.

ALMEDA. I'll find Babe.

If she won't take me now, I'll hustle the pick-ups til she'll see me again.

I'll play to eat.

JEAN. You want it that bad.

ALMEDA. I do.

JEAN. Then you ought to take this.

(**JEAN** *offers her the burlap bundle.*)

ALMEDA. Jean, you should keep it.

JEAN. No, you're going to make a living playing basketball.

You'll need the one you've got a feel for.

(**ALMEDA** *takes the bundle.*)

ALMEDA. Thank you. I don't know what to –

JEAN. Al.

Remember me for always.

(**ALMEDA** *nods. They hug for a long beat.* **ALMEDA** *holds on as* **JEAN** *holds her out at arms' length to look at her.*)

JEAN. (*cont.*) Now, run wild.

(**JEAN** *steps back.*)

Go out and play.

(**ALMEDA** *smiles and nods, then turns to take the oxblood ball out of the burlap bag. When she looks back to the spot in which* **JEAN** *had been, she sees that she has disappeared.*)

(*The light grows a little brighter.* **ALMEDA** *inhales and looks out to the horizon. Then she dribbles the ball.*)

(*Blackout.*)

End of Play